Large Animals

Large Animals

Jess Arndt

Catapult   New York

Published by Catapult
catapult.co

Copyright © 2017 by Jess Arndt
All rights reserved

ISBN: 978-1-936787-48-7

Catapult titles are distributed to the trade by
Publishers Group West
Phone: 800-788-3123

Library of Congress Control Number: 2016940540

Printed in the United States of America

9 8 7 6 5 4 3 2 1

To Litia Townes Perta, for the fire

Contents

Large Animals

Moon Colonies

In the morning the waves glowed like uranium, a deep sweat coming up off the seafloor. It was beautiful but it was nerve-racking too, being that close to the future.

Then a bloom of moon jellies drifted in, their tentacles dragging behind them like purses. I thought it was a sign, some kind of big money omen, but Joelle said we should get ready to move on, start trucking north—where we were really headed.

For the past month we'd been "down beach," less than a mile from Atlantic City, camping out in a mail-order bungalow belonging to Thea's sun-shriveled grandfather. Me, Thea, and Joelle—we'd had it to ourselves—one hundred square feet of no electricity, plus the washed-out fire pit and jack pines.

"I want to try the Taj," I said. "I have that feeling."

That feeling had done well for me so far.

At least it had kept Thea and Joelle in tallboys and blobs of Coppertone, and that day, for lunch, we had lobster from a shack that seemed too legit to be real—a wonder that in between the boardwalk's Shoot the Gimps and the constant grind of tattoo joints we'd found J'ean, the Lobster Man, two samples from his morning's load of big 'uns in his baloney-colored fists.

J'ean was headed north too, back up buggin' lobster on Eastpot.

"New Jersey lobster?" said Joelle. "How shitty does that sound? I mean, by comparison."

J'ean just shrugged. "Goin' to breeze up today," he said through the slice of his hand.

That put an extra volt through me. I loved storms. I turned toward the ocean. It was still August but now the waves looked like sandwich foil that had been crumpled up and hucked away. I was in a hurry. The boardwalk was an ongoing line of cracked wood; it stretched forever.

"Let's take a cart-pusher," I said.

A rickshaw cart was extravagant, but we were leaving soon. Joelle had a job to get to in New York—she referred to it vaguely without offering even one giveaway detail—and Thea's sister had just popped out twins into the Grey Goose–saturated swamps of western Connecticut.

Babies! How wild. We bought them pint-sized T-shirts and joked about their names. *Felix. Maude.* We loved them already as an idea.

Thea was a week late for her obligatory nanny gig. No biggie, she said. That was Thea. We'd been something two years ago, had been so looped on pints of tequila and what she called sloth weed that neither of us remembered much. The non-memory was connective.

BEACH! Thea had said on the phone, a month earlier. She knew I was depressed in New Brunswick. Bored and hot. *Joelle's here,* she said. *You'll like her. You'll see.*

But Joelle was different. My crush now seemed like something I'd been born with. Plus Joelle was smarter than me: her brain had that slaughterous left hook.

"The Taj," I said, aloud.

The long line of cart-pushers stretched toward the casino action. It was a casual, twenty-four-hour kind of job. We passed two snoring against the cracked vinyl benches of their contraptions but the next guy along looked scarily awake.

"I haven't slept in three days," he said.

"Awesome!" said Thea.

"Really!" he promised.

He must have been fifty, a meth-head probably. I assumed they all were. His hair was sticking up but he had a nice face.

There was a haze over the boardwalk. I couldn't tell if it was the heat or the breeze up, sucking aloft those clouds of sand. I felt clammy pressed in between the two of them. A line of sweat slurred along my chest binder. There was a time when I was sure I would get surgery, when I stayed awake late staring at the plaster wall. I'd made an appointment with the surgeon even, checked the box: payment plan. A giddy, raw feeling. How could it not mean change?

The cart jerked forward. I stuck my palm between Joelle's jean shorts and the seat. We hadn't been alone together since we first mashed faces two nights ago, which meant sex with our clothes on, a bunch of fingers, punk shots at best. We lay next to

each other in the violet half-light of the bungalow's only room—
not caring much about Thea but pretending to care, keeping
sort of quiet. We were accelerating particles about to separate.
Soon we'd be peeled apart.

"It's just a body," Joelle had said, when I bucked her hand
away from where she was trying to insert it.

"Sure," I'd said, bleakly.

"Okay, yeah, it's internal. But it doesn't have to be *domestic*."

I rolled away from her, from the king-sized futon the three of
us shared, our only furniture, the raft in the middle of our floor.
I tugged the sweat-stained material back into position over the
slack mounds that on good days I pretended were giant pecs.
Joelle leaned down and put her thumbs against my temples.

"It's Thea, right?" she whispered. "You're so shy!"

"Yeah," I said.

This had nothing to do with Thea, but then again, I hoped
it did. I was a concrete bunker pretending to be a friendly,
all-access picnic area. I scrubbed a small pile of sand across a
floorboard. Joelle was naked more than not.

The next time it happened, she stared at me from far away.

"Why *don't* you just cut them off?"

Our cart neared the strip. First was Bally's. Bally's had a Wild
West front, with sheriffs and hookers painted all over it. It was
ridiculous but secretly it turned me on.

"Yee-haw," said the cart-pusher.

"Get a room," said Thea, elbowing me.

My body was trying to wedge itself underneath Joelle's. It
must have been something floating from her pores.

Two teenagers ran out of the air-conditioned saloon doors, flinging off their Nets jerseys when they hit the hot. I stared at the bank of their bare torsos. There was a sink in my old studio building with a sign hanging next to it. "Black Mold," it said, a Sharpie-drawn arrow pointing down into the dirty plastic interior. My painting summer was gone and not much to show. I'd drawn exactly one still life: an oyster and a flattish grape.

"Can't go in Bally's anymore," said our cart-pusher, nodding it by.

We were cruising faster now.

"When I started this job I was pants size thirty-eight," he huffed. "Now look at me, I'm thirty, thirty-two!"

He wore his expression like a founding father. Someone you could trust.

In the Taj Mahal, gold chandeliers spaghettied from the ceiling, gaudy and awful. I played *Frontier*, drawn into the vortex of radioactive desertscapes and howling coyotes, and then immediately hit it big on MJ's *Moonwalk*. A thousand bucks on my second spin, zing zing zing! "Billie Jean" exploded from the speakers while a rocket sprayed MJ with moondust.

Joelle sat next to me, smoking.

"Let's get a room," she said.

When you score like that the hospitality staff comes over—they don't want to let you alone. We stared up at two managers and a tired-looking hostess whose sole job it was to get me drunk and playing again, tout de suite.

"We're very happy to have you here, Mr. . . . ." They trailed off. "Very happy."

The manager in charge smiled olympically and handed me a plastic card.

"We've put you in the Chairman's Tower," he said, "ocean view."

"Yeah sure!" I said, chewing my lip. I was sweating but I wasn't sure why. Everything was the same, but outside it looked very dark.

"Do you have any tequila?" I said.

They hustled it over to me in a plastic Taj cup. It must have been a slow day. Thea had evaporated, probably reading at the bar, and I thought about strolling over to her and swinging her around as the skirt-thing with legs she'd recently been wearing swooped. I'd always been comfortable and drunk with Thea, half-blind, in a warm cave.

Then Joelle and I were in the elevator, grinning, pressing all the buttons at once. I clamped my voucher ticket. A thousand bucks, we said back and forth to each other. A thousand bucks! It was that free kind of money that you could do anything with. Joelle wanted me to cash it in so we could throw it all over the bed.

"Just for fun," she said. "*Then* you can call that surgeon."

I thought about the old Biggie video, the stacks of cash flying everywhere, the helicopters, the epic yacht.

"It's only fifty twenties," I said. "Is that really enough?"

Our room faced east as promised. There were smudges on the mirror and cigarette burns pocked into the heavy carpet. We sat at the little coffee table and I stared at Joelle. My neck felt prickly. She'd gotten tan, really dark. She was Italian. Her

Italian-ness and double-jointed thumbs seemed like perfect chemistry. She wiggled them idly as she smoked. Now the water looked like a series of yellow planks and the sky was hot and gray. Joelle took off her shirt in a motion so convincing I wasn't sure she'd ever had it on. I wanted to ask her about the job in New York but stopped. The room felt thick after all our time out on the beach. The wall-to-wall. The so-far-undented carpet space near my feet where we should fuck, astral wand, blow our minds et cetera, after, and only after, we did it in the shower and on the ample bed. I twisted my plastic cup of warm tequila.

"I should get some ice for this," I said.

In the hall I began to walk toward the elevator. Soon enough, I was back downstairs. Grit had settled on the machines in my brief absence. I re-fed in my ticket and thought about moon jellies. They were see-thru but vacant. *It's just a body*, said Joelle. On the screen, the aliens and their queen, Michael, were changing colors and shapes before my eyes.

The $1,000 became $963. A minor subtraction. I would've spent it anyhow. Plus, I still had *that feeling*.

When I looked up again, it said $815 in the lower left corner. I should find Thea, I thought. She'd love this. I wanted to show her the whole ticket, the $1,000. I increased to MAX BET. Wind blammed against the boardwalk-facing plate glass, the windows of my chest.

MAX BET MAX BET MAX BET.

There was no one around; the place seemed practically evacuated. This is how the game works, I told myself. If you quit now, it's got you, you're a real loser. In front of me, craters opened up in unison, spewing confetti. Each eruption seemed like a sure win. But still the left corner dwindled. I began to think of Joelle, topless in the room. It seemed dumb that I had left. Worse than dumb. Abyssal.

I knew I should take the ticket out, but I couldn't. The lizard part of my brain kept saying: the next spin is the one. I had another tequila. Then a few more.

I knew a guy back in Albuquerque whose foot went numb from a skateboarding accident, then turned an angry celery color. Eventually they had to cut it off. He was okay through the operation but in the recovery room, goopy with anesthesia, he became obsessed with wanting to keep the foot. He was going to taxidermy it from toenail to ankle, he said, and freestyle it into a lamp. The surgeons gave it to him reluctantly. After all, it was *his* foot, what could they do? He stuck it in the freezer and five months later, when the taxidermist was ready, he got the lamp.

"What happened next?" said a voice next to me, a bun-sporting granny zinging away on *Miss Kitty*.

"Nothing happened," I said. "He was a real weirdo."

"Well, did the lamp work?"

"Yep. He said it had a nice homey glow. But then one day he came home from work and his dog and the lamp were gone."

"Did he put out an APB?"

She hit a *LITTERFEST!*, and the siren atop her machine flashed like cherry Jell-O.

"He did," I said. "Except it was just part of him that was missing. A missing foot report. They found it down by the viaduct, the place the accident had happened to begin with."

I paused for effect.

"Well," she said.

"It was gnawed to pieces," I said with relish.

It reminded me of a dream I'd recently had where a shark circled my chest hungrily and I felt relieved.

The coins from LITTERFEST! stopped ringing and she began to hum.

"Lord, I should cash this," she said.

She flashed me her sleeve hem and no fingers, just a cauliflowering stump atop her old wrist, the skin fused to itself in tight folds.

Then she was gone.

I was sweating swimming pools. What's that horrible sound? I thought. But it was just the deafening silence of *Moonwalk*. I stepped into the bejeweled elevator with an awful chewing in my gut. There were a million times I could have stopped. It wasn't free money. It was a chunk of something.

I fiddled with the floor buttons but this time they were sticking in their slots. I was there in the mirror—my sloping body, my very own continental shelf. They hadn't found the dog after all, that was the sad part. It had just loped off. Already I was begging Joelle to forgive me. On the closed face of the elevator doors, a prayer from Emperor Shah Jahan floated over a flat Taj Mahal:

The sight of this mansion creates sorrowing sighs;
And the sun and the moon shed tears from their eyes.

But in the room, Joelle was missing. The cleaning service was vacuuming up our nonexistent mess. I sat down on the bed.

"He was in here," said Joelle's voice. She was talking to Hotel Management in the hall.

"He was just sitting there like a total SOB." She moved through the gold-trimmed doorway.

"Oh," she said flatly, "it's you."

Apparently some skuzzbucket had entered our room while I was gone. Had sat down on the bed, just like I was doing. When Joelle came out of the bathroom, he was flipping the channels.

"This asshole?" said Hotel Management, pointing at me.

"No, not that asshole," said Joelle.

Now she was livid.

"I've charged some things to the room," this new Joelle told me. "Majorly $$$ things."

"Uh-huh," I said.

"But you can cover it, right?"

"Uh-huh," I said.

The TV was still on. The news anchors were saying things like "level two" and "hurricane" and "South Carolina." Was the Chairman's Tower wobbling?

"Don't leave," I said to Joelle.

"This is still our room, right?" I said to Hotel Management.

I went in search of Thea. She appeared, a bright hole in the gloom, at the Rim Noodle Shop bar.

"You look like a train wreck," she said. "No. More like a train who, for no reason, stopped and then tipped over. What happened to you?"

"Two tequilas," I managed, to the barman. Boy was it dark.

"It's a hurricane out there," I said. "A big one. If it's not here yet, it's coming."

"Uh-hm."

Thea seemed skeptical, but I sensed a radical shifting of things: a new world order.

"Thea?" I said.

I had a decision to make but I wasn't sure what it was. When I leaned over and tried to put my mouth near hers she hit me.

"You idiot," she said. "You idiot idiot idiot. You *NERD*."

I took the same cart-pusher back to our bungalow. Rain globbed against the sand. I was hoping Joelle and Thea would be there— at least, I thought I was. My skull was hot.

"Found you!" he said, elated.

What a great new life without sleep, I thought. We rolled on. Caesar's, Trump, Tropicana.

"Can't go *there* anymore," he yelled at each one over the thump of the tires.

"Why's that?" I yelled back.

"You drink?" he said.

"Who doesn't?"

"They kept handing me screwdrivers, buying me stuff with Visas, Mastercards. Everything premium, I was happy as shit!" He paused. "Shit went south real quick."

I nodded. "It usually does," I said.

"I was running," he said, "as fast as I could. But after a while, I just stopped. I got right up into those pigs' faces. I really wanted to know."

The light was gone. Between the drops, the beach stretched out, a fossil of itself—all wear and cruddy ridge.

"Know what?" I said.

"I mean, somebody had to have the answer!" said the cart-pusher, doing his best George Washington. "They had me by the short hairs, I was bawling like my life depended on it, but I had no idea what for!"

At home, Joelle and Thea were on the phone, which meant crouching in the bog bushes behind the cabin. It was the only place with reception. I followed their voices and the blue cellular glow.

"It's Thea's sister," Joelle informed me, glaring. "The twins are sick. Their fevers are climbing past a hundred and four."

I lay down on the sandy wash. It was intuitive, canine. The lower to the ground I got, the better. I wanted to pull Joelle down on top of me and bury my face in a hunk of her rain-sticky hair.

Thea covered the phone with her hand. "I can get a flight," she said. "But there's a weather advisory? I have to go now."

"Can you help her?" said Joelle, looking at me hopefully for the first time since *Moonwalk*. Joelle had money but it was all glommed up in something, her father probably.

I thought about my empty wallet, my art school economy. I scrubbed the ticket out of my pocket and handed it over slowly.

"Three dollars and twenty-four cents?" said Joelle.

I'd painted the Taj Mahal once in a class. My dome had a nice full onion shape but those moon-facing spires that lined the central tomb had confounded me. Somewhere around their midsection they'd rebelled—sticking in every direction but up. My art teacher threw out his hands.

This is all about Love! he'd said, pacing. *And Sacrifice! You're so terrestrial. You're scared to leave the ground!*

I looked at my spires, their tips lopsided and heavy, tugging down toward earth. *Boobs*, I'd thought. I was too embarrassed to say my Taj was already on the moon, that's how I'd understood it in the first place.

Contrails

I WAS GOING TO CHANGE EVERYTHING. THE FEELING BEAT through me with its smothering pulse. I'd been waiting to change everything for an eternity, thirty-one years, a very long time. I was sure this meant what I was going to do would change very little. Still I could think of nothing else. I'd spoken to the surgeons—or at least one surgeon, a rising star with a Mad Hatter's throne in his condo-ish waiting room. The chair spooked me.

Now I was going to do it.

As the date approached, my preoccupation grew. I'd purpose-fully trap myself sideways in empty windows or mirrors, trying to chase down the future me. I had no idea what to expect, except hopefully: Lothario, pleasure-seeker, and, of course, famous author, household name recognition, writing books that made not just people *but their cells* cry.

This period was full of lasts. Last time go to this or that

restaurant or take the E train to therapy, last four a.m. car service in sway of alcohol-induced feelings, last optimistic but still shittily fitting shirt, last time to see so-and-so before the change.

I was also having send-off conversations in my head. If I'm honest they mostly copied the one I'd already had with my therapist.

"Well, goodbye," she'd said. "Next time I see you you're going to feel so motherfucking free!"

I was embarrassed when she said it.

"Ta-da!" I'd said, bolting for the door.

But it had become a model.

I went out to dinner with S. at Thai Me Up. We sat inside at a plastic outdoor table and drank tiny glasses of water. We had sheltered a heavy flirtation once and now it was settled but seeing each other still kicked up dust clouds.

S. was back with her ex and, as she put it, having *the best sex that they could have*, which left a little trapdoor swinging open. Staring over her perfect shoulder, I scanned all of the possible pitfalls, inadequacies, faulty equipment in their "dynamic" and plugged the data into a mental Excel sheet against mine.

Certainly I measured up (surpassed) in many ways—but there were other activities, behaviors, proclivities that, if I was radically fair, might not have favored me. I brushed them back. The fact remained, I was about to change everything—and who knew who might pop out on the other side?

Our food came and I sucked at my Thai iced tea like a jungle guide pulling out viper venom from a stump. Things had become very sharp. My actions were bolder and less tethered to anyone I had been or anything I had ever done. My body did not yet work better but I padded around in it as if it did, hoping people would notice.

"What did you want to tell me?" S. said.

A gosling surfaced in my stomach and shook its greasy head. I ducked down, my neck broiling. I looked at the well-mopped tile floor. Were my New Balance dirtied permanently? I wondered, or could I, with some soap and water, return them to like-new?

"Ummm," S. said, "hello."

My hand was doing that flutter. I pressed down on the stem of my fork. Hurling it across the room felt like my only option—there was no way I could get the squirming tines up off the plate to my mouth.

That night I couldn't sit still. My earlier behavior was not an example of how someone about to change everything should act. I should make some calls, I thought. I pulled a half-finished Modelo from the fridge—someone had jammed a napkin in it—and scrolled through my address book.

The window was open, the elm leaves flipping up, showing off their white bellies. I stared across at the dark apartments and air conditioners from my position on the third floor opposite. For an instant I felt aware of a great resistance, something bigger than me. Night made me dissolute like drinking did. Put a stretchy space between my synapses—pushed on my legs or arms until there was no body, just black ether lapping at milky shores.

I called V.

It was east to west so it was okay. One a.m.

"What do you want," she said. She was at a party. Things crashed jovially in the background.

"I wouldn't have picked up," she said. "But I'd erased your number and thought you might be the pot dealer."

"Oh," I said. "Do you have a minute?"

I was only interested in calling people I had slept with or dated, people who if they knew I was about to change everything should want to give me send-off bon voyage and all that happy landing et cetera et cetera jazz.

With V. I was going very far back, but in my new accounting, it made sense that the women who had known me longest should have the most time to adjust.

"I've been thinking about giving a little send-off party," I said. "Or maybe I mean like a final viewing."

"A what?" She seemed suddenly disattached from the phone. "No no, it's not him," she said.

"A final viewing. Before I change everything."

"Are you doing a lot of drugs out in New York?" she said. "Diet pills? MDMA? Mushrooms? Glues?"

"You thought I was the drug dealer," I said. "As in *you* called *him*."

"A final viewing is what you give someone who's dead," she said. I heard glass breaking. "Are you dying?"

"You'll be the first to know," I said.

I opened another Modelo, gazing into the refrigerator's chilly rib cage. When I was a kid it occurred to me that I might be a very corrupt person, a murderer even. Just the word, every time

I thought it, gave me a hot little shock. One day the knowledge was shoved between the other things I knew about myself—okay at soccer, desperate for sugar, a loner. I was nudging a body out to sea, as I had at sleepaway camp that famous summer when a decomposing shark washed up on the beach near our tents and all night it was my job to push the rubber flesh back against the tide with a board.

This terrible power made me shyer, more self-effacing. I was very concerned with keeping myself in check and performing the daily rituals that I manufactured so that others would be safe.

I described this one night to a girlfriend, T., who often let me get drunk and cry and rip up serviettes against this bar top or that bar top and tell her just these sorts of things. But she wanted to be a social worker so I didn't feel too bad.

"What if the fantasy really had less to do with your capacity for destruction and more to do with saving everyone?" she said.

I didn't know what to think. It was true that as soon as a "dark thought" occurred, I threw myself into the solution, eagerly murmuring words and moving objects around in the dirt.

Her number wasn't in my phone but after some digging, I pulled out an old journal marked "2000." Just its battered face gave me the creeps. I extricated the number with tweezers, three-thirty a.m. Central Time.

Her wife answered.

"Fuck you for calling so late," she said. "You know we have kids, or you would know if you called more. Did you finish your book?"

"I gave it up," I admitted, but she had already put down the phone.

I turned my receiver up to max.

"No one, hon, it was just . . ." she said.

I could hear all the way through their Chicago apartment. Their parquet floors and the hot breath of the babies next to them, their macaroni fingers clasping and unclasping.

". . . yeah, same old thing."

I listened to them sleep awhile in the dark.

Jeff

BOY DO I WISH I LIVED IN THE PENTHOUSE 808 RAVEL. WHEN-ever I walk by its ample surfaces, its hacienda-style balconies and black moribund palm trees, a shiver runs through me. I learn things by relation. For example, now I write *moribund*—it sounded plausible, but who knows? Better to have said *doomed, expiring,* or how about *at the end of one's rope?*

The windows are always dark when I cruise down Hamilton Avenue, carefully peering up at what might one day be mine. Picturesque barely cuts it. The oily swath of the Raritan glimmering so meanly. Like a zipper? "Man vs. Machine," it says on the bordering fence—a relic of times gone by. "Man is machine," I mutter. But even that thought is years late, barely worth repeating.

But Penthouse 808 Ravel has promise. Shag carpet. Doors that shut heavily. I have sexual feelings about Penthouse 808 Ravel. Ligature feelings. Relational feelings, knots, bandages. I want to look at the floor plans. Even now I can smell the mimeograph ink that reminds me, in a sharp inhalation, of last night's freshly snuffed-out sky.

I work across the street at the state university. So does Sheila. I think that's a great name. If I had a pet I'd name her Sheila. My knees have gotten a little sweaty now, bringing her up. Soon you'll want to know what the deal is. *What's up with you and Sheila?* If I murmur nothing, you'll squint and frown— *It's okay*, you'll say, *you can tell me*. Then slowly at first, but soon enough, as if an ambulance is screaming behind you, you'll get irate—*Why'd you even bring her up? Now get out of the lane, and let the poor fucker drive.*

I can't imagine ever needing an ambulance at Penthouse 808 Ravel. Sure, it's a decadent place. There will be a series of indulgences. A party where all of us from the state university's English department show up in sweaters on top and nothing down below. Not cardigans either. Big hairy sweaters, mohair— or, better yet, horse. Quaker stuff. Holy Roller stuff. At Penthouse 808 Ravel each window has its own private balcony, a place to air your parts. This is also where they keep the moribund palms. I can just picture it, some new gawker walking down Hamilton, taking my place even, getting misty-eyed about Penthouse 808 Ravel, and then bang! between the palms—it's Buzz Snyder from Vic Lit, showing his rolls.

Yes, I did have dinner with Sheila. Yes, I did approach her on false pretenses, the false pretenses being: Dear Sheila, I am on my last nerve, I'm begging you please give me some great advice about these lesbian circuit parties I keep attending and the women who are always loitering outside my Subaru Outback

1999, begging for a ride. Sheila was happy to do it, she said. *More than happy to do it.* Which brings me to another question. Why Sheila and why not the state of Nevada? I personally think the comparison is obvious.

But this isn't even what I wanted to talk to you about. There's something more pressing, something I call "Jeff." Let's forget about Penthouse 808 Ravel and Sheila, travel back to before the state university, before my name had "Part-Time Lecturer" attached like a plume to the end of it.

The first time I met Lily Tomlin she was so nice. She called me Jeff. "Hi Jeff," she gushed. I'd been her bartender but she only drank water. "Hi Lily," I blushed back. What a warm handshake, what a firm and knowing grasp!

"Wow!" my pal said from her barstool. "Is she progressive or what? She didn't even bat an eyelid!"

"I think she just thought my name was Jeff," I said.

That was the only time I met Lily Tomlin, our solo tête à tête. But Jeff stuck. Actually Jeff had been trailing me for some time. My box was stuffed with Jeff A_____ bills and junk mail. Jeff was horrible, like an insurance salesman. That's how I pictured him—thick neck, coarse red fur sprouting from his ears. I knew he wore a Mormon-white short-sleeve button-down and that his lips had zero color but were the texture of banana peels stretched tight.

Jeff gave me the heebie-jeebies.

How to then explain the small satisfaction at reading my universe-generated new name? I mean it's very similar, first two letters—same. Next two letters—not same, but double, which leads me to an auxiliary concern: is *f* intrinsically more masculine than *s*?

It felt like a consolation gift. Like the universe saying, *Hey, sorry about that boob thing. Oh, and we kind of flubbed it dividing the world in half, and language as enforcer of binary divide? Yeah. Not to mention bathrooms. OOPS. But gosh, well . . . here's Jeff.*

Other days the cosmos didn't speak to me. Things seemed more mundane. Jeff was just . . . there. But it couldn't be some clerical error. Lily had said it too, and she wasn't linked via paper trail to the unglamorous annals of my bill-paying life. Still the Jeff thing continued. I called to reschedule a surgery again and the receptionist was effervescent. "Hey Jeff!" she bubbled.

"No no," I feebly protested. She seemed let down at the news. People liked Jeff.

Plus—if, as I correctly guessed, we do not live in a benevolent universe, then there was only one conclusion left. I was purposefully muffling the last two letters of my one-syllable tag; I was prank calling my own name.

My father always told me I had marbles in my mouth. Wait, no: "*Put* marbles in your mouth," he said. "Put marbles in your mouth every day and talk for ten minutes. It's essential to be c-l-e-a-r."

Marbles, how 1950s, like I just had them lying around. But I admit, thinking of it now sounds kind of nice—smooth hard gobs of color rolling around my gums and tongue. What would Sheila think of that? *Hey Sheila,* I'd say, *whatcha doing this Friday? It's Jethhh.*

Sheila again. I can't get away from the "now," from the state university and her office ladies, her Scarlet Knights. The other day a famous writer came to talk to us. They'd even made a movie out of her book. She gives a packed reading and at the end she says she wrote the book because she wanted to talk about something that was unreported: male rape.

I agree with her. Of course I do. Then, rushing toward the transit stop, I miss my train. No problemo. I want a substantial drink. Sitting under the trestle in a chain BBQ joint with carbon copies of my students jammed around me, my mind drifts. What's going on at Penthouse 808 Ravel? I wonder. I've never seen anyone enter or exit the place, but I'm sure it's a pleasure picnic—deluxe fun. Just thinking about it feels good. I order fries and sauce. A guy to my left is flirting with his girlfriend. "That asshole," he says about someone else. He rubs his finger down her hair. "I should just fuck him in the ass."

I snap shut like a clam. It's a hostile universe and these overgrown kids, my best and brightest, are all violent offenders with newly thickened arm hair, whispering sweet nothings into their sugar-soaked Texas teas.

Still an hour until my train, everything true and mean around me. It's even sleeting; I see it through the glass. I go to pee. A big BBQ joint kind of door. Shiny tiles. At the sinks, a familiar squadron of girls who giggle as I approach. In the mirror—oh god, it's Jeff. Hair like a scrub brush. Perv gleam in eye. Flat dry fingers holding wads of receipts.

Sitting back on my stool I am sweaty and red. The rapist and his girlfriend are waving sticky ribs at each other and canoodling. Jeff, Jeff. He needs a lesson, someone to give him a firm talking-to. I imagine bending him over, his pleated pants going tight. No, it's okay! Lesbians can talk about fucking men in the ass, can talk about teaching them a lesson, about giving them a "firm" talking-to.

You get it. Extra points if they're straight and white, which Jeff of course is.

For the next week I dream about Jeff. He begs me to do all kinds of humiliating things. *Tease me about my cuticles*, he says. *They're so flaky and hard. Make me eat cereal with no hands straight from the box. Tell me I have a bad memory. Put my head in a bidet. Now pull it out and put marbles in my mouth.* In my dreams, these activities and more take place at Penthouse 808 Ravel.

Then it's spring break. I go on a wine tour. We stare into the big sweaty vats of red. "Wine fermentation," the expert says, "happens when all of the individual grapes explode against the walls of their bodies." *How nice*, I think, *for them*.

I ask Sheila to dinner again. This time to a Mexican joint—well applauded, et cetera. First we park and saunter along the banks of the Raritan. Or at least along a pathway that occasionally comes in view of it.

"What's going on with your circuit-thingies," she says. She has on open-heeled flats that slap-slap as she walks. Her wildly weather-inappropriate footwear seems promising.

"Oh nothing," I yawn. I really haven't been getting much sleep with all my Jeff dreams. They're getting worse. The things I'm doing to Jeff are ugly. "Actually, Sheila," I say. "This might come as a surprise, but my Subaru stops for you."

Slap-slap. And that greasy river, god it looks good.

Over chicken chimichangas I pop it to her. "Do you like Lily Tomlin movies?" I say. This will be my segue.

"She hasn't been in that many movies," says Sheila. "She's pretty much a TV actress if you ask me."

That night I can't sleep, period. I play the rest of our date over and over in my mind—the salsa verde that splotches onto my pants, the way Sheila drops her cactus-decorated napkin down. "Oh," she says, touching the bag of air, the wasteland of nothing, in my crotch. "Oh my," she giggles, "you're *large*."

Poor Sheila, I've been waiting for women to tell me this my whole life. Is this why I pay the check silently and drop her off three blocks from her house, even though I know full well where she lives? Sleepless, I watch myself push marble after marble into Jeff's ever-expanding ass. I'm hurting him. I know I am. Somebody help him! I think. But he has everything.

Jeff.

It's spring now. The blossoms are out. I don't walk on Hamilton Avenue anymore. Sheila and I ignore each other in the photocopy room. She giggles up to Buzz Snyder without mercy.

La Gueule de Bois

IN THE CITY WHOSE SOLE MONUMENT IS A COMICALLY
upturned syringe and whose light is not *like* gauze but *is*, it was
as if I'd borrowed all my language from an obsolete guidebook. I
kept saying things like:

> "I understand only station."
> "My dear Mr. Singing Club! I have pig."
> And most often, for no reason that was clear to me—
> "Stay on the carpet."

Still, these expressions allowed my transit, and the strangers
whom I was always meeting seemed to accept them with good
humor. Actually, they completely ignored my lingual botch
jobs. I was sure they knew I was talking nonsense, but since they
stubbornly refused to admit it, I was left alone in a strange cloud
of non-meaning that smelled, of all things, like linden trees.

For the last week everywhere had smelled like linden trees. The blossomy funk was inside the clubs where I'd been hiding out, traveling all the way down to the pervasive always-popular dark rooms, and back up, along the river, clinging to my skin and to each particle of wet air. It was summer now, the trees were telling me. Did I care? I was interested only in all-night parties.

But this morning, something was wrong. I flopped up from my mattress and crawled to the nearby mirror. My hands were pale screens. My hair had remnants of old fruit in it from some bacchanalia or another. Oh no, I moaned, looking.

I'd woken up with the wooden face.

I regarded the mirror again. There was no getting around it. A flat broad block—it must have been five inches deep, a foot wide, a foot high—was my only expression. To make it worse, there was no grain in the wood at all. It was only thick and smooth and hard and hot.

But what had I been doing with my face? My heart was racing. Only, my memory, like my face, was entirely blank.

I did my best to get dressed. My T-shirt neck refused to stretch over the wood slab. I sat at the bare window, completely unformed, squeezing a glass of water. Below, near the falafel shop, squat dogs sped turds onto the ground.

Does it go on like this? I thought. On and on forever? It was hard to tell the hour. Here the sun was a flea jumping out of the night's thin batter; it never stayed down for long.

* * *

All over the tiny apartment that I rented weekly, beer and wine bottles, empty, hunched. I believed they'd accumulated over time but then again, was it possible there'd been a party? Luckily I'd discovered a metal box on my corner, whose symbols led me to believe that it was a recycling bin. Simple enough. Open the slot and toss your bottle down the hole.

I shoveled myself into a duffel coat and picked up the nearest glass armful. See, I could still participate, be useful. I stepped onto the third-floor landing. Near the banister, an old stove nestled as if vagrant—it too removed from its home. Suddenly I was pushing my foot against it.

"And that's for loving me!" I said, bashing away. "And that's for not!"

Behind me, the door to my flat lunged closed, locking me out.

"Never mind," I insisted.

I pounded down the stairs and kept on, doggedly, out onto the street. I could quickly tell it wasn't morning but here it never is. Here morning is like an unkempt relative we never visit. Sure, they want us to! But who likes visiting?

At the corner, I opened the slot and tossed in the first bottle. As it passed my fingers I saw its label, cryptic—a variety I'd never heard of let alone bought. If I'd been drinking *that*, well. Anxiously I leaned forward and then farther forward and even farther down—my wood face was almost inside the chamber.

My oxygen was constricting. I wanted, more than anything, to hear the gorgeous bell of that mysterious wine tanker smash. Yet there was no sound.

I shifted my load.

Something about that endless chasm reminded me that maybe I was mistranslating my predicament. What did I know about here and there, definitions, attaching things together? *La gueule de bois*—"the wooden face." The stiff plank I now wore on my neck. Could it also mean a face of woods? That seemed freer. Thinking along those lines, I began to breathe again in short quick bursts, feeling a certain soft bark grow over my cheeks and the possibility of one teenage moosling, obviously a symbol of self-worth, stepping knock-kneed between my many trunks.

I took another breath. When I'd arrived in this strange city from New York and set up camp in the minuscule bottle-polluted flat overlooking the canal, I'd been fixated on one thing only: to avoid pain at all cost.

Was this that?

Now I glanced in King Falafel's window with fresh hope: *be gone.* But between the cone of shaved meat and my reflection, the plank persisted. A big chunk of hard wood clamped onto my shoulders and underneath it, the rest of my body Gumby-like by comparison, barely there.

Just then a man passed me beneath the lindens, a man I may have recognized. I set down the bottles, smoothing my jacket.

"Hey, was it you?" I called out. I was sure that with this added obstruction, I was speaking only more gobbledygook and that he would continue on.

Instead, he stopped. I leaned my weight against the metal box that held the bottomless hole.

"Yes, it's me," he said.

Me, me. And who was that? His eyes were small oceans and the skin around them was fiery red.

"As you can see, I have the wooden face," I said.

I touched the surface, rapping my knuckles to demonstrate.

He paused thoughtfully, and as he did he turned sideways. Meeting his lake-tanned neck, I was struck with a squall of recognition. How could I forget that last night he and I had been in that bullion pot of a swimming pool (itself housed in a makeshift club), that between the synth beats he'd grabbed my ankle and laughed. *We're all so happy!* he'd said, as his urine ran down my legs. *We're all so happy, we're peeing in the pool!*

The memory swam up from the chlorine abyss and I felt a something tugging beneath it. The peeing had only been at the night's start.

"There's nothing wrong with your face," he said, interrupting my memory's possible rebound. "Albeit you look a little puffy from this party you had."

Gold light clung peach-like to the swarming clouds. This was the clearest conversation I'd had in months. I wished I were anywhere else, walking along the canal. I shifted my feet and my toe clodded into a bottle that fell, bursting.

"I'm not here by accident," he continued. "I left my cat in your apartment and I'm here to pick it up."

But now I was adamant. I could feel my chin bobbling, or trying to, through the uniform block.

"My face," I said.

It was *impossible* to me that he could not see it. I was sure, suddenly, with absolute certainty, that this wooden face is what

33

I had been searching for all along. That it was the necessary scaffolding for my mush-like feelings that would not recede, even here—an entire Atlantic away—but kept always slopping forth.

"Chi Chi," he said. "My cat."

I scanned backward. Impossible, a cat. And I was locked out of my flat anyway! At last I had found a boundary and could be firm.

But he hauled closer to me still, brushing gooseflesh onto my arm, and as he did my stomach gouged and I felt us skirting around that club through a high-fenced pitch-black park, pausing under a linden tree whose low-hanging buds—his fingers on my sodden thigh—my lips troughing out sideways—the megacosm shearing past us at mock speed and spunk-like green linden smell of yeast and caving in, of being fucked all the way up the middle—a river the color of currywurst that I kept—

I wanted to be another person.

"Come with me," he said, trying to gather me toward King Falafel. "At least a beer."

But my head had begun to throb and my vision sworl. There were grains now, too many of them to count, as if I were looking through tissue. Around us it was growing dark. I saw that out on the street, in clumps or pairs, many others were having this same conversation.

"*A beer?*" "A beer." "*A beer?*" "Yes. A beer."

I knew then that I would have to travel home.

Been a Storm

"IT'S AROUND BACK," HE SAID.

I must have been staring. I'd recently turned a bend in my life where staring was okay, unobjectionable. On subways, for instance. I no longer pretended not to look.

I read it again: "Crawlers in the Cooler."

"*Around* around back," he repeated.

The black marker behind his head scrawled out—wormy too. He had those free teenage muscles and his Nikes up on the counter. Whenever I did that I spilled something. Like this morning: coffee everywhere on my half-done papers, which quickly transferred to my badly ironed shirt and more yelling on the phone about directions, flood weather, town names I couldn't decipher.

Now I was late to something you couldn't be late for. The 278 traffic smear, the blades of water in the ditches along the road—no excuse. I slapped my keys on the counter. From a dislocated speaker above the Coke case Stevie Nicks was singing that song that's too sad to feel with your whole body. It was *past capacity*.

I have always, she said. *Always.*

"You're going to Dawdson's, right?" he said, nodding. "Storm fish. They been catching a bunch."

Meanwhile a girl in a knee-length hoodie was trying to get him to come outside onto the porch.

"'Scuuuuse me," she said, snapping her fingers in front of his eyes. "For a smoke. *Please!* It's good for you."

"It's not good for you," he said, staring back at me, "it's *smoking*."

She snapped again with more elbow.

"Just lemme help this brah," he insisted.

I'd stopped here why? But I couldn't sit in the car anymore with the radio dipping out of reception and the June green so wet it was blinding me. It was hard to remember that brah/bro/dude/*him* didn't mean anything in particular, didn't mean stud, winner-at-life, or even, most basically, attractive. There were ugly brahs. Dumb brahs. Brahs with bad breath and boring thoughts.

Eggs floated eye-level in a scummy mason jar. A half-split watermelon slowly saturated the wood counter with its gestational juices. Over the weekend I'd been at the beach. We drank cans of sudsy beer then tried for the sandbar. The swell was enormous, whipped up by something offscreen that was maybe now arriving, days later, with the rain. Just out of depth, I'd press my foot down on the bar as securely as I could, trying to hold it there before the next wave, always bigger, knocked me off.

* * *

The screen door whanged. The aisles were empty except for the musky insinuation of wet that had been following me from New York.

"But you fish, right?" he prodded.

He flipped a Bic across his knuckles.

I heard life grinding on the road outside. Me in time-jelly.

He expelled air past his bottom lip as if: *well, which is it.*

Deep down I'd always been a pleaser. Or what was it exactly? Wanting the other person to be right about me. Relieved, I'd happily grab on to whatever solution or version of self they offered up.

"Uh-huh," I said. "Lots."

I walked past the sign that read "toilet" with a handdrawn smiley face and x's for eyes, the raw plywood walls of a storage room. Invariably (usually within minutes) my new identity became impossible to upkeep. Desperate not to reveal their blunder, I'd stutter and second-guess myself, trying to diminish my contact with whoever it was until I was monosyllabic or, better yet, gone.

"Keep heading," his voice followed me, agreeing.

The gravel lot behind the store was empty too. A retriever was wagging and scratching between the gouts of mud. Some part of me had been kinked up in the car. A wand of light seemed to swivel out of the Dumpster and inject the tubby clouds.

"Bait," read another sign, then an arrow.

Everyone writes a fishing story sooner or later. There's that Carver one, or is it Cheever, where he disappoints his dad. And what about Gordon Lish, with all of those blowfish stuck on the string that's really just an old drapes cord?

I mean, c'mon, boyhood fifties crap. I did have fishing stories. Father stories. On boats I had a free pass—my body was totally employed, I barely noticed it.

The girl was huddled next to a rust-tracked Igloo. I'd just watched a Swedish drama where a woman's body showed up in a similar chest freezer. Half a body actually—the bottom, now unusable half.

The Igloo coughed or clunked. "They're in there," she said, pointing. "The worms."

She was wolfing down her cigarette. She reminded me of someone I'd regularly seen at coke parties in SF.

I shrugged. I didn't want to see them.

"Why'd you come out then," she accused, "if you don't want crawlers?"

She was pretty in a way. I considered calling the dog to me and rubbing it. Panic unrolled somewhere between my adductors and belly. *What about the dog?* Who would mix his raw food, wake up early enough, or, when he became too difficult— continue to watch him?

"Cut the BS," she said. She rolled up her sleeve. "See this?"

The UCONN sweatshirt bagged in huge folds around her thin elbow. There seemed to be a runty scar. I bent my head toward her skin and inhaled some kind of tuberose scent that will always make me think about locker rooms; girls with coils of wet hair.

She slammed me in the ear with her flat small fist.

"What the fuck?" I said, recoiling from the sharp beak of pain.

"Crawlers!" she said, opening the freezer top. Icy steam poured out of the cooler box. "Yeah *right*. I know you came back here to gobble his cock."

The tuberose was drifting around the parking lot, getting stronger. Those gym class years I had dreamed of getting hit.

"What?!" I said, trying to rub off the purpling mark. "I'm like a . . . *you know*."

She assessed me. My shiny uncreased shoes and too-new pants. The duffel bags bulging on the conveyer belt under my eyes.

"Where are you going anyway?" she said, as if I was just now coming into focus. "A funeral?"

I put on my best face. "I'm going to Dawdson's," I said. "Give me twenty killers, okay?"

Back on the freeway they livened up to steamy car temp, twitching their tube-like bodies on the seat next to me. "St. Mary's Church on Hillhouse," the directions read. It was the wrong thing to bring. Way worse than nothing. I fed more dirt into their Styrofoam cup. I'd been apologizing for it my whole life but something had to live.

Shadow of an Ape

San Francisco: July something-th, 1860.

Phew, night's kaput! I tell the canting ceiling and its mysterious mushrooming water stain. My mattress is thick as a single sock. My pillow, paste. I stare into the room's armpit, suddenly dry-mouthed. That hairy space—*there—behind the chair?*

Four floors below, some stupid clatter. Outside, same fog blob for sun.

"Señor Pinkie," the landlady accuses my keyhole.

I pull the raggy coverlet over my head.

As soon as I signed her terms—*"no boot-slop in rooms, no succor with whores, no smoking vile poppy"*—she delivered her litany. How the California waterfront's *stuffed* (she relished the word, beating my name in her ledger book) with shanghaiing outfits—"crimps" ready to sell you off to the nearest seagoing vessel, poisoners trafficking in chloroform-drenched cloths and knockout drops.

As if I wasn't from Valparaiso! (We locals call it Valapai.) *Mush*, I'd said, finger to my lips, ending it. And now what's she want from me? Taste my breakfast stew?

She moves off down the row. Ugh, I hate to miss things. Shooting up from my punisher, I'm already at the washstand. I blink around again, searching for the regular male chests inflating—bushy and dank—but for once, I've scored a single slot.

Lately luck's on every side. Me, Sr. Pinkie, shipping via registered packet all the way up from the greatest port in Chile. And the formal drama of my departure, the crying, red-faced Espacio, the attention of the uniformed guard? Back in glossy Chile I was popular and full of potential, a made man with a ticket north.

This town is so crammed up I'm stuck at "Every Man Welcome," a pay-by-week at the dullest end of Dupont. At least five blocks down everything's modern and cutting edge—"Terrific" Street with its groggeries and drugstores, its cow lots whose habitués are female impersonators, its lace curtains and monte tables.

I lean closer to the spotty glass. Face bones nicely excavated, my pores jump at me like fleas. I keep my face bare *bare*.

All that skin up close makes me woozy. In Valapai there had been that roast chicken dinner (a chicken the size of a dodo) and tin cups of pisco (they kept pouring themselves) and the fresh-from-Frisco stranger who'd made a beeline for me— diving over the knock-kneed table to whisper the mathematics of a gold-mining operation north of Placerville, California.

Prospering, he'd said, practically foaming.

Then cuddled me to him, drawing it all out like he was relaying a recent conquest: here, Pinkie, are the tender arms, here, the protected entrance, *now hurry over here the dynamite KABLOOEY!*—another small vein to probe.

I dampen a cloth in the basin and try to cool myself.

Find Butt Riley, he'd insisted, pressing the lode claim of a lifetime to my palm. Jeez god, his heat was immense.

I rush down to breakfast; the corridors are narrow, a series of collapsing tunnels punctuated by numberless identical doors. At least the canteen's marked. *Ahem,* I compose myself, enter. Every Man's eyes skate around me as if I'm not here. I'm small, 150 pounds with my gut out, but I stand up straight. I have reason to—*twenty acres, my own mill site, nuggets the size of small shits.*

At the window a sign reads: "Every Man Hungry." Exactly right. It's only scrap sausages. I prod what's handed at me. Two pale witch's fingers surrounded by a plateful of grease.

I have a strong feeling I'm staying at the wrong locale. "It ain't like the 'Jewel of the Pacific,'" I address the room. "It's no Valapai."

From what I can gather the rest of my dorm-mates belong to a not-soon-enough departing vessel called *Zoila*—it rhymes with *voila?* So what.

They all, every one of them, have mop-like beards and saucer eyes. *Zoila* is from the Gulf of St. Lawrence, Quebec, a place I would *never* visit. But here we all are, in the doilied-up dining room together.

I lower my plate to a table where three Zoilites, identical in every way, bunch.

"You ever been to Valapai?" I open. But sure they have! It's the only way round the Horn.

Still the Zoilites are unmoved. Plus their dishes are licked bare. I'd better tuck in, I think, before these nutsos help themselves. I scarf my sausages, my chunk of toast, my pickled egg. Then I reach my second chunk of toast across and drag my neighbor's plate.

"You don't mind, do you?" I say, nudging his well-shaped shin with my boot. "We do this kind of thing in Valapai."

I can't stop talking about the place! Something eels around. I hate Valapai, if only for a second. I touch my back pocket, the one with the claim shoved in it. Of course I pull it out, caressing the oily script with my finger. Today I'm going to find Butt Riley. *Rugged*, the stranger had called him. *Overly tall.*

"Dear guys," I say, rolling a cigarette, "saying adios to Frisco must be tough. I know I was glum when I left Vala . . ."

But the damn clock moans. The Zoilites nicker and draw back their chairs. They move in unison, always.

"Pals," I say, "how about a light for my smoke?"

Their backs are to me now, a desolate line made by the French linen of their shirts. We should all wear the same thing, I offer semi-silently, if we're going to live like this together.

Later, a man's big toe is reaching and reaching and reaching up from out of a stone well. A taste in my mouth of zinc or clay. Now my body's roaring awake against the seam of my pants.

Unbuttoning, I milk myself into the blanket's wooly face, glancing around without interest.

My memory is full of bald patches and gaps. Only, I must have returned from breakfast up the wheezing stair to a Zoilite's dormer because here I am: alone, but in a Zoilite's room, surrounded by his strange Zoilite stuff.

I push at my skull. Had I, groping even though outside it was day, wavered at *his* doorknob instead of mine? Then, when it brushed against me—*that terrible thick feeling*—jumped not out but *in*?

And what if!

It doesn't change facts. This sludgy ache tells me I've been more than sleeping. Somehow over breakfast they dosed me, dumped me out cold. I thrust open the window and stick my head into the night. Below—all the sounds of evening, the vigilantes hounding and tamale vendors begging for my stomach's dollar and a bright steady tonging that I just now noticed going roundly to the east. It must be the mountains. They're tearing their new machines through the hills! The sound falls just outside my knowing. Each time I think it's done a distant hammer waits a second longer, then tongs again, making me start.

Every Man Welcome, I assure myself. Every Man, *that's me.*

I sit down on the Zoilite's bed and wait. Images of Valapai swim through me at great speed. Can you believe the brand-new funiculars lofting us up her teeming hills, the gorgeous tuba-shaped women and their endless train of "invitation-only" fiestas, the popping sound a sugarcane made when I crushed open a stalk between my molars? There was one party in particular—

I'd taken Señorita Espacio, "the Bullfighter," they all called her. I'd been forced to by our hosts. That first meeting, my adversary's (as she quickly became) calves sparkled in her encrusted stockings. *Espacio, enchante!*

It was a miners' gathering at a palatial ranchero up in the jungly plateaus north of Valapai. They were rough guys, miners of explosives (some said aphrodisiacs)—i.e., saltpeter. Tons of it, clearly: the party-givers were rich. It was the night before they were about to make for the shriveling Atacama Desert and I was drunk already, I must have been, because I remember stumbling over the marble doorframe on dumb feet and everyone laughing and laughing.

Give Espacio a little pleasure, my female host had said.

We drank cases of just-off-the-boat Italian licorice-smelling Strega and inhaled steaming bowls of cazuela. At one point I was instructing them in the polka. At another, my throat was clogging, I was eating something very dry. After my fifth tiny glass of that sticky yellow heaven I thought briefly about marrying Señorita Espacio. After my seventh, I mumbled something to her, something that lifted from the carriage of my body with great weight. I was teary then, it was such a sad story. After glass eleven an oversized golden horn butted out of her forehead.

I pressed her hand to my cheek. Her palm felt like clotted cream.

"You'll have to excuse me," I said, by way of exiting.

"It's probably better that way," said the señorita, giggling. "After what you've told me so far."

But what had I said? I felt like I was sitting on an anthill. In the following weeks my agitation only grew. Soon I was pursuing taverns that were always farther afield, places I was sure no one would know me, barrios of ill repute—tin waterfront shacks if I'm honest—with buckets on the sawdust floor to collect the gallons of that cheap grapeskin we pissed, or was it only the rain? Regardless, I was sure that if I got cavernously drunk then I would make that same obliterating confession again. And since I would not stop drinking—impossible in Valapai—I'd better not risk the shame.

Down on Dupont, the gum trees chatter their dry long tongues. The white of the moon makes me choke. These Frisco streets are large, twice as broad as the tight wends of Valapai. An alien something could take me, I think. *Extraterreste: of or belonging to another.* Then wonder why I thought it. Get a hold of yourself, Pinkie.

I do not try the door. I don't have to. I've heard of bunches of poisonings like this, even stood out on Columbus Ave. and broadcast them myself:

"Sailor, don't take that drink! Don't touch that muffin!"

What this town is famous for. Anyway, I'm sure the door's bolted. So which guy is it? I wonder, fantasizing about my captor. Try as hard as I can to picture the Zoilites, they all look exactly the same—those beards jumping out from their faces and flying around the room like kites and those wide blue plates they wear for eyes.

An even uglier thought hits.

Robbed! I'm sure my pocket's been pierced and I'm sitting on nothing, nada. The feeling's so strong I don't check for my claim. I don't need to. Instead I tear at the guy's room blindly, sobbing for Valapai from my boot-bent toenails all the way to the tips of my ears. All of Frisco can hear me but I don't care. What a careless bitch she is too, to leave me alone like this in the attic of my ruin.

Come to think of it—if I track it back, everything leading up to my current noose is predicated on my whispered confidence to Srta. Espacio and her scoffing haughty tone. It was in one of those anonymous tin shacks (a particularly sweaty one called Tropezedo) where I met the man with the magic claim and the "friend" Butt Riley, who I am now seeking, am this very day supposed to (in the flesh) meet. In Tropezedo my appearance was porous. The place was so squeezed full of nobodies, I spoke to anyone I could find. *Yes*, I'd said, reaching toward his robust torso for the claim paper. *Leave my dear Valapai? Bend over and grab my ankles? Yes, yes.* Of course the stranger planted the idea of "Every Man Welcome" in my head too, although I had much nicer joints in mind. Why, I wouldn't be surprised if he was a Zoilite himself—it's not so hard to shave a beard, after all!

Then, as if sensing I've come to the abrupt cliff-end of a thought, someone knocks.

"Who is it?" I say.

A scuffling sound against the doorframe and something thick—body- or barrel-sized—dragging up and down the hall. They're out there parading like usual.

"Come in," I say, making my voice boom.

He opens the door. His hair shines with water or oil and he's parted it down the middle so that when he bows it, I can see the white shock of his scalp. His hands are bundled in front of him. It's his room but, can you believe the gall, he seems to be waiting for me to invite *him* in.

"Well, come on," I repeat stiffly, descending another octave.

I now see he's got his left hand clamped on a bottle of 'bou, the only thing the Zoilites drink. It's a harsh kind of liquor mixed with syrups and wine. I'm thirsty, of course, but angry.

"Harassing me's hardly the best use of your time, is it?" I demand. "You have my claim, you mugger, and the hammers are going out there all night and all day, making men rich. What are you waiting for?" I glance around his room—the sheets in sticky ribbons, the drawers sitting dumbly after vomiting their insides. "Butt Riley?"

But the Zoilite steps around my outburst easily, in fact, he barely seems to notice. He perches on a plain wooden chair, uncomfortably close to my position on his bed. Our knees, damn him, dance. I throw his blanket across his thighs. *Cover up*.

"Do you know, in Valapai, there are apes in the hills?" I start. I'm not in fact sure of this, but who is sure of anything, anymore. "With big ape faces and big ape hands and they drag their fists like this [I demonstrate] in the brush."

There you go, Pinkie, I think. You're winning this.

The guy hasn't said a syllable; it's like his mouth is full of paper or pitch. *That's tree's blood!* I try to continue with my story but can no longer find its pulse. Only that, in my final weeks in Valapai, I believed a shape moved next to me, the shadow of the ape.

I'd like to tell you more about it but that's all I know: at the corners of my vision a figure lumbered. When I turned, it was gone. Worse, I had the distinct feeling that it was not the ape itself who was tracking me, but only the dark spot it cast by being alive.

The Zoilite uncorks the bottle and takes a wet gulp. He waves its mouth end at me.

"And now you want me to drink," I hear myself saying.

What choice do I have? I'm desiccated. Those distant sausages were just cheap salt packed into old casings. I snatch the spirit from him, wipe the neck, and pour the stuff down.

It's hard to say what comes next. The room seems to fill up with Zoilites, or is it just the same guy, multiplying, getting bigger? Then we're outside, tossed from "Every Man Welcome" onto the bumpy face of Dupont. Marching beside him, I feel exactly as if I'm being carried aloft on his broad Zoilite shoulders and I begin to see the streets as channels flowing toward some terrible outcome that I've been streaming toward ever since Tropezedo, the stranger's crushing odor, the moldy peeled cane walls.

Again I'm filled with all the old worries and complaints. I'm sure behind the bungled ape story, another one lurks. One that will permanently expose me.

Kerosene lamps bob like buoys in the pulpy dark, stretching a long way off. A few guys swim past with their collars up but by and large the avenue is empty. I'd expected the Zoilite to keep offering the spirit, but he's tucked it away, the miser, just as my thirst picks up. In Valapai things soar on well past dawn. Where's the fun anyhow?

Frisco, honey, you seem grim.

Just then a foghorn comes on, low and gassy. At first land I'd cozied up to it but now its monstrous bellow fills me with nervous, chilly vibration. If I felt more myself I'd punch my subjugator in the beard-smocked throat and jump on the next packet to Hunan or distant Boston or even, as the foghorn implores: GO *HOME*.

Impossible, my brain howls. I've been robbed. Still, I try to keep my head.

"What streets are these?" I say. But we go on and on in engulfing silence.

Finally he puts his hand up. In front of us, instead of wharves—cannibalized sloops and hay barges, half-sunk, filled with trash. I scuff my foot. I much prefer the broad eucalyptus-lined avenues near Dupont. You know, Stockton, Kearny, the Devil's Acre, yes, even Sansome! This is a desolate drop-off, rimmed by semi-built factories. "Dew Drop In," it says above the door.

I don't laugh. Why would I? It's a shack with a stovepipe, that's all.

The Zoilite stands listening in the door's breach, smoking. This guy is implacable. Here we are out in the City of Speculations and he wants to take me to the dumpiest joint around.

"Is this your best choice?" I say. "In Valapai we have Bertie's, Flora y Fauna, A Little Bit of Sol-o." I tick off my favorite spots.

Keep Tropezedo out of it, I tell myself. "Christ, I didn't *want* to come to Frisco," I moon louder and spit.

Sure, when I was on the jetty, on dry land finally where I could see those brown hills coaxing me to play my claim and someone yelled "You aren't fine till you're in Frisco!" I'd felt a small bang.

But if this is *all* she has to offer? My mouth jerks free of my brain. Espacio! *What had I said?* I'm lost in the murk, but her crystal stockings, her legs of ice, won't let me go.

I remember (with fresh sprouting horror) the cramped letters I'd written her, the names I had called her, the threats I had made. Wasn't it true she'd been making her rounds? Bowl after neighborly bowl of cazuela? Dinner after blabby dinner? Sharing my news?

Extremes like these drove me to Valapai's social citadel: the courthouse. *So Romanesque—with its uniforms and columns!* My eyes were still burning from the long nights at Tropezedo. But what choice did I have?

Better if I unclothed her before she unclothed me.

"Fine, fine," I said, announcing myself to the clerk. "Here I am. Let's clear this thing up."

But I shuddered when I entered the interior office. The colonel in charge was a Valapai party man. In fact, it was *his* ranchero I'd been at—he'd headed up the saltpeter miners that condemning night. Now his boar-like face charged at me from behind his desk and his eyes glittered from wet folds of skin.

"Señor Pinkie," he breathed. My presence seemed to inject a localized pain.

"Señor Pinkie, it doesn't look . . . *so . . . good.*"

These were a surgeon's words before he tossed away a healthy leg, or a finance man emptying your account. You dunce, he'll want a payoff, I thought. After all, Espacio was his wife's friend. I reached for my wallet. Ten reales. Twenty reales? How much could he expect?

I paused.

Hadn't she hoped to infect me against myself? Then wasn't it normal to launch a campaign? Violent, sure. Push a dick through a garden window? Well, if it was open, why not? I shook my coin as the colonel moaned sadly. A few grubby pesos fell into my palm.

"Señor Pinkie . . ." he said again.

That breathing! My neck prickled. Its sucking sound made a familiar gurgle in my brain. But then his face unfolded and widened and the well-boiled nubs of his teeth snuck out from behind his lips, making me wince.

"Espacio, she was . . ." I started my defense.

"Brandy!" he exhaled. Suddenly we were faced with two shiny tumblers and a half-full resinous carafe.

I wasn't sure whether to sit or stand so I hunched over in front of him on his llama hair rug.

"Do you remember how you made us writhe around," he said, "how you made us pray to that whore Hathor, show our ass puckers, out there in the yard?"

I nodded to please him, but if I'm honest, my mind (besides my half-cognizant and exhausting encounters with Espacio) was blank. Hathor, goddess of miners, I found myself mumbling. *Thou art the Mistress of Jubilation, the Queen of the Dance, the Mistress of Music, the Queen of the Harp Playing, the Lady of* the Choral Dance, the Queen of Wreath Weaving, the Mistress of Inebriety Without End!

He bent his head and then swung it up as if catching a scent.

"We crept under the vines together, Señor Pinkie," he said. He crashed his tumbler down and the brandy slugged over. *"Eh?"*

Then he seemed to change tacks. His eyes swiveled to the ceiling.

"Dammit, we scoured for those hidden caliche beds. But the Atacama ..."

His face was terrible now, cracking into little pieces.

"... was *dry*! ... *Hahahaha*, get it? The Atacama was dry!"

The Zoilite crushes his cigarette under his boot and shoves his hands together, blowing off the cold. He smiles at me, at least, his lips twitch.

We enter a dank passageway. Lamps smoke up from the gravel floor. The walls are tight. Coral flowers cover the wallpaper, oozing like tiny decapitated heads. From the outside the shack looked infinitesimal; now I realize they've sneakily buttressed it from the back.

We press in farther. The passageway slopes to a steep grade. It's colder. The walls flanking us are no longer wallpapered but seem to be bleeding: hacked out of sedimentary stone.

I know where we are. Buried under the city where they'll wrap me up like one of Tut's mummies and trade me off for a dollar to any old passing ship. He must have a fistful of chloroform. That's why he'd been listening so closely, to make sure we were alone.

"I'm guilty!" I beg, grabbing at his linen frill. "Do what-all you've come here for!"

My memory of Espacio has ruined me. I'm sure I've performed even more desperate things that are only waiting to catch me in the dark. Even at "Every Man Welcome," I've stirred the pot. Haven't I hated the Zoilites? Reported them to the local squads? As if I was hotter stuff?

I stare into the gloom. "At least give me some more of that 'bou, man, so I can get good and poisoned," I say.

But even that he withholds.

I pull a claim from my back pocket. Then more, claims with Zoilite names on them even, waving them all at his retreating shape.

"Hey!" I shout. The fogs finally lifting. "Butt Riley!"

He stops. His beard, its mammoth overhang, seems to take over the cave. I'm nearly trembling waiting for him to speak. His mouth opens. He shakes his head. Finally—the transaction will take place.

"It's 'Paraiso, man," he says. "*Nobody* calls it Valapai."

What can I do but get down on my knees and crawl first one way then the next? Until I'm crashing through the roble trees again and that filthy brush, away from the colonel's ranchero with their colossal laughter.

Pinkie, they sang after me, horribly pantsless. *Señor Pinkie, Se-ñor!*

I hid below while their search fires smoked, my chest ballooning hard and hot, my poor arms suddenly so long my knuckles rubbed the ground.

I don't know why I do the things I do.

Now I slouch into the tunnel's sand. *Frisco, honey, I'd love to touch you, if I could just get ashore.* But down here, dammit, it's just like Valapai.

Third Arm

ALL FALL I'D BEEN CARRYING AROUND SOMETHING THAT wasn't mine. Or maybe it was carrying me. Regardless, it kept me company. I often dragged it out from where it cowered and tried to look at it. When that didn't work I fed it alcohol.

It's not like I had a lot of time. I was busy with a new job as vice-vice-something at Queens College, New York—it was a job they were making up and so none of us really knew what I was doing. Plus I was bartending down the block from my Bed-Stuy apartment, and then there was "the writing."

The thing was more important than all of that, it must have been.

Sometimes it made me shout until my voice went hazy and erased. I liked being without a voice, it was a complete relief. This went directly against what my healers at the Authentic Process Healing Institute told me: that I had a blockage in my throat chakra and had to talk. It was after one of these particularly long sessions that I got into my mostly crumpled Datsun 510, lunged on the engine, and began to drive. It was November so the poor air quality that swiped my windshield felt not only atmospheric but, in its opacity, right.

I had a five o'clock meeting with an assistant dean. We were planning a suicide-prevention week that was supposed to pre-empt the inevitable depression of the season. In our meetings thus far he'd been sprinting past gung ho and I was invariably hungover, a combo that caused the team of us to skip forward many logical steps and ended with me in my small basement office calling companies like Maxi Adult Bouncing Castles, inquiring after the price.

Traffic was bad. Something in my session had made me antsy, my Authentic Process Healing Institute Corps Leader, as they—refusing actual names and the inevitable attachment that came with them—liked calling themselves, had been in a provocative mood. What if everything you think is authentic about yourself is nothing more than affective glare? she'd said. For instance, that "thing" you carry around. It's bullshit, right? And when the winter line comes out you realize Uniqlo's selling them too?

Not if H&M gets it first! I'd whooped. Then had spent the rest of the session in the long hallway, cycling between the vending machine and the bathroom.

The news droned from the car radio: stocks belly flopping, a Trump rally, another one—nothing I could catch on to. I unbuttoned my jeans, dug my hand under the band of my boxers. I only liked jerking off while driving—otherwise the sincerity of the act completely killed me.

I surveyed the gag of cars on the BQE. How many other commuters were fishing for pocket trout? Waxing the carrot? The terminology drove me nuts. Okay, so what do you call sitting against a steering wheel with all that freeway filth below you, imagining you have a cock in your hand? And about the cock: it's yours, you made it, but you don't care about it too much either. You aren't that dumb.

But I was too restless to make my body work. Plus a thingy in the catalytic converter had broken off and in the rearview mirror I could see a death cloud spewing out from my exhaust pipe. Other drivers were glaring and pointing. Now not only was I practicing self-abuse on the freeway, I was single-handedly causing the oceans to swell, the atmosphere to wimp out, and the defilement of forests so virgin they were irreplaceably ancient. All of it: me. I turned up the radio, mashed my cheek against the glass. Instead of feeling cool the window was brick hot.

"This is Bubba the Love Sponge on Cox FM." The speakers gasped back to life. "Okay, hunters, *listen up.*" Great, I thought. Following the squalling trail of a Zeppelin song had stranded me on a Tea Party bandwidth.

"Do *you* know what *you* were doing in 1840?" Bubba coaxed in baritone.

Easy one, it was my favorite era. "Oregon Trail!" I shouted. "The wagon broke an axle and Sissy's got the cholera!"

Lime green pixelations on a field of black.

```
Date: June 30, 1840
Weather: hot
Health: poor
Food: 242 lbs.
Next landmark: beer?
```

"Well, if I know you like I *think* I do," Bubba drawled, "you were probably shooting bear." He said it *bahr*, I knew that word, I'd been there last night and part of this morning: my abandoned socks, jacket, pocket gunk spread between the bed and the toilet when I woke up.

I listened absently as I drove down 495. It had been all over the airwaves, one of those stories announcers couldn't put down. For the first time in two centuries, and only for this weekend, we were free to spray bullets at Connecticut's black bears. I wasn't an animal lover. They're probably dangerous, I thought. Besides my antipathy to Bubba's voice, I didn't much care.

By the time I got to Queens College, a pudgy dark had descended. The big beech trees rattled above the PTL parking lot. On my phone, a series of texts from the assistant dean:

You're late.

Now you're really late.

I find it a big bummer that you don't care more about what we're trying to do here.

Honestly it makes me worried about you.

And finally: *Call me when you get it together?*

He couldn't help himself.

Whenever that is.

As I walked to the lounge, I wondered where it had gone wrong with us. There was a night a few weeks ago where we had been the last two at a post-reading wine reception. Both single, both ambivalent cooks, we crouched over the fig puffs and mini quiche that I fervently wished contained chunks of ham. Had I tried to tell him about . . . ? It was likely. September and October had been so bad I'd been practically hibernating but the FishEye merlot had woken me up.

"The problem's the women I'm into," I'd managed, massaging the hollow above my clavicular head like my healers had instructed. Confessing to my habits made me feel wide open, part of the universe's radiant core. Talk, I thought, talk.

I shuffled my feet around meaningfully, waiting. But something was sticky. When I looked under my shoe there was a bit of gore.

"Oh god," I said. "Look, gore."

"Gore?" he said. He dived down toward my shoe and reemerged. "It's an edamame pot sticker from that platter." He pointed. "It's not *gore*."

Salman Rushdie, the season's big-ticket reader, had just exited the room and to be honest there'd been a kind of stampede. It was possible that food had been crushed. But as I inspected the fleshy blob, I became more and more resolute. "Gore." The department always looked down on us creative types anyway. Thought we were all liars and hacks.

Now I flicked on the fluorescent lounge light and stared over the scene. Microwave, mismatched chairs, multiweave carpet with a mid-nineties pattern made from some impenetrable armor-like fabric so it seemed barely worn. No assistant dean. It was a Friday night and Queens College was a commuter school. I didn't want to be here but couldn't stomach getting back into the Datsun, rolling home.

Maybe I should go to the library? I wanted to find that story that Burroughs had written when he was a kid: "Autobiography of a Wolf."

Don't you mean *biography*? his teachers had prodded him.

No, he'd said. And again: Nope, no.

My phone wiggled in my pocket. "Going to tell the ass dean to fuck himself," I said aloud.

But instead of him, it was a Connecticut number, one I'd erased a million times.

La Cocinita at eight?

Sweat basted me. We'd driven each other so crazy that I couldn't even remember when we'd seen each other last, that file was sealed. Three-day screaming matches (her idea), degrading meet-ups where I'd beg for her attention but *only*—I knew it as I was doing it—so that *she* wouldn't have to be alone. But now another memory was strolling back to me, some horrible blip of drinking-induced magnanimity where my brain said to my typing thumbs: .

Yeah, sure, some margaritas? Great.

I went into the bathroom and shoveled water over my head and shirt. Then I jogged to the car. If I left now I'd be late but tolerably late. Plus: I didn't care what she thought anymore.

* * *

I approached the passenger-side door. It was an embarrassing form of self-chivalry my car enforced. The driver's side could only be opened from the interior lock. But something was sticking between the door and the frame. As I pulled the door open, it plopped onto the ground. I bent down and flashed my phone.

This piece was apricot-sized and, unlike the Rushdie gore, seemed mostly made of fat. But there were darker globs too. It made me think of a bar I'd been to near Joshua Tree. I was driving the 10-east. The structure seemed cool and friendly against the mid-afternoon blare. I gulped two beers and, in the bathroom, seeing no option besides a urinal, crouched with my shoe wedged against the door. From my position I eyed my pubic hair, then the darker seam that was usually camouflaged by curls, with fresh but falling hope. Gross. When I sat back down on the barstool I realized I'd been staring at a mostly disintegrated human foot floating in a formaldehyde-filled jar.

"Colombia?" The bartender seemed unsure when I'd asked him where he'd gotten it. "No, *Hawaii*," he said. "Or Nam."

"Actually eBay," he admitted later. "You'd be surprised."

"Huh?" I said, snapping out of something.

"I could tell you were a writer," he continued, "so I had to get my story right."

"Scientists have proven that matter doesn't exist," I said. "You see a foot but when you get past all that skin bone squishy stuff et cetera, nothing's really there."

* * *

Traffic had cleared and I accelerated over the Triboro. I couldn't stop thinking about the assistant dean. His life seemed pitiful to me. I couldn't imagine what he'd had to get home for. Or why, when we'd been talking and drinking wine, he hadn't understood that my problems, and in fact this *was* my problem, came from outside of me.

WELCOME TO CONNECTICUT, the sign said, bulging into my headlights' view. On cue the wheels thumped in misalignment. La Cocinita was a hole. A taco joint that smelled instead of fryer grease. I remembered a faraway night when I'd popped a tire on the curb and she'd psychoanalyzed my flaws while spinning the iron over the hub nuts. *That's talent,* I thought.

"What's wrong," she'd said later, "what's wrong?"

It was raining very softly. My vision turned diffuse. Coffee. These injections of anxiety always came accompanied by a chasm-like dip. "An emergency brake," my Authentic Process Healing Institute Corps Leader told me. We'd been working on it together to little effect.

The Merritt Parkway only had a few gas stations but I'd seen a REST STOP AHEAD. I drifted along the gentle curve of the exit. When sleep did come, it was so abysmal that each morning I woke feeling worse than when I'd gone to bed.

The phone jackhammered again. I cranked the stereo dial in response.

". . . shoot out a nice bahr skin," shouted Bubba.

My eyelids were thickening. My narcoleptic friend once described it as a seduction so druggy you'd never want to resist. No problem, I resisted nothing.

Suddenly drooling against the Datsun's steering wheel, I was gone.

When I woke, the rest stop stretched around me. Someone who looked like the assistant dean was mowing a path between the bathroom sheds. Dark lawn spit out behind him. *I had to be awake.* I didn't believe in dreams. They were forbidden in writing class, my students all knew it—immediate, pitiless F.

"You're such a control freak," the dean-ish guy shouted, looking over his shoulder. He was wearing a headlamp. *"And that thing you were trying to tell me about, what a joke!"*

I felt like joining him—laughing back—but as hard as I shook, no sound came out. I gestured to the mower that I'd lost my voice. He kept mowing blindly.

Closer, I told myself, lugging my body.

Only—something was blocking me from his sight. Trees. I was standing in a giant fir forest, thickly needled branches brooming my sides.

Something else was wrong. My pulse was ragged. My gut hurt. Then it gushed at me: I was hornier than I'd ever been. Feeling the mower near me, sensing him completely, cell by vacant cell, I was going to bust, discharge molten spunk, cave inward, fuck anything in sight.

Was this how everyone else felt all the time?

I lumbered from behind the branches, my head swinging down. Black fur dragged with me. The thing I'd been carrying twinkled everywhere.

"DEAN," I bellowed. My lip curled without meaning to.

Terrified, he steered the mower engine between us.

"Just let me shave these down," I begged.

I stared at my paws and their gore-smeared claws. I knew if I touched him I'd turn him to human paste.

But I was so full of love.

Together

WE HAD IT TOGETHER BUT WE ALSO HAD IT WHEN WE WERE apart. We got it in that comedor in Oaxaca, we both agreed. Or maybe it was that little town, just a few palapas actually and a beach with a deceptive number of black dogs, called San Angelino. But it's also quite possible that we had gotten it on the subway. Don't forget about a head of lettuce! our naturopath said. They caravan those heads in from anywhere imaginable. And water these days—it's no good washing with it.

We made a list of what was now okay and what wasn't. Sugar, yeast, all the essentials—*out. Enter*: lines and lines of herbaceous esophagus-jamming pills we swallowed noon dinner and night.

"It's not so bad," you said. "We weren't into that kind of junk anyway."

But who could tell? What we were and weren't into? For instance, Bloody Marys at Giondo's, what about that? And occupation politics—was it possible our parasite was affecting those too? Before, we'd been heavily committed: gotten arrested even, clubbed by the militia-era NYPD.

"Let's take it back to where it came from," you said. "Niagara Falls or the Jurassic period or what about that town you like, *Boring*, Oregon? It really feels like it came from there."

What we shared had sticktuitiveness. You had to give it that.

When we looked it up online the definition said: "one who eats at the table of another," which seemed kind of cordial, so 1950s, like a neighbor plus misshapen apple pie dropping by.

But who had neighbors like that?

Ours were more like that guy we knew, Raif, who on his way home sloppily inserted himself into our kitchen, slogging through our sole bottle of scotch, probably shoveling coke up off the back of our toilet seat without offering any, probably crying even—before wheeling away again into the splashes of light and dark, the leafy trees and trash that made up our block.

We had it together, this relative of giardia partying in our now shared intestinal tract, *but* we reminded ourselves—*we could have picked this thing up anywhere*. The lack of fault was comforting. Plus the parasite wasn't all. In our Greenpoint yard hard pink asparagus-like weeds were erupting everywhere, pubing skyward with a level of tenacity I no longer recognized.

When I was young I knew that everything was sentient and I was capable of great harm. Moreover, I knew that things should not be separated—that pairs, no matter where you found them, should stay intact. Under everyday pressure, that feeling had gone underground. Now, looking out at our yard, a spray of turf between the parallel avenues of McGuinness and Manhattan, it swam up again.

The stalks seemed so invincible, thrusting through the heavy metals and constant turnover of Popov bottles that made up our soil. Should I inject them with syringefuls of recently outlawed weed killer, as RAT574, my new buddy in the underground chat rooms, urged? The kind that gives everything gooey eyes? I could do it at night beneath the pale gray dome of light pollution we lived under.

Or what if I let the stalks showboat, have their time in the sun? Nothing else was growing.

"Make a choice," you sighed. *"I don't care."* You'd been saying that a lot lately.

Still I was locked in an intractable standoff. It distracted me no end. I often stood on the pitched steps, dolefully. Then I would descend into the dirt and snap off their waist-high heads, pinching the magenta frill between my finger and thumb. That barely slowed them. Even pulling at them did no good. It was Japanese knotweed, and, as you liked explaining, their roots flanged out at the base like butt-plugs.

Around that time I got fired from the Baltic, a ramshackle tavern on a drifty block of Avenue C, left smoldering from an older, more terrifying era. It was huge, draped in once-regal green felt, with smoke stains that stippled the floors and ceiling like Sherwood Forest fungus.

"Too bad about that Big Fuck Up," said my boss, Terry, a pleathery fag in white Keds. He shook my hand in a friendly way.

I'd been there for years, dutifully slinging Yuenglings. But I didn't have the heart to fight for my job. I knew he was trying to get rid of us, his loyal few, so he could bottom for the Pinnacle Corporation. In the last month their goons had come around nonstop, checking the place out while Terry twisted them a fortune of cold beer.

I faced the barroom for the last time. *Ooooh I feel good I feel good I feel good*, said Donna Summer. Gerald sat on his stool with his long braid dangling behind him, drinking E&J. I walked over to him.

"Well," I said.

He grimaced. He'd been tall but now his body was cinched up.

"I hate to go home," he said. Gerald was stuck in the eighties. His nightmares were endless hospitals. I wedged a twenty under his glass snifter.

"Not tonight, pal," I said. I wanted him to keep getting good and drunk.

"Try to remember," I said, arranging his lapel. "We're safe now."

I stood on the Bowery platform and waited for the late-night J train. My gut yowled. Our parasite was a new and mysterious development. It was gross, but it gave us something to talk about. I glared warily at the track. Did everyone want to jump in front of the subway as much as I did? Not necessarily to die, although that was, of course, likely. *Help!* I'd shout. Someone would come. Still, once the thought occurred, it felt impossible to resist. Persuading myself that everyone was gripped by the same mania—a mania so regular it was boring—made it less awful when I shrunk from the inevitable approaching train, scrunching my eyes against the finishing blow.

That night I sat for a long time in the dark of our kitchen, looking past the window's reflection, out into the yard. Then I went to bed as usual. Our apartment was so narrow it seemed as if we together were Jonah, inhabiting the "inner whale." You'd disagree, scoffing into your hand: *as early as 1520, Rondelet knew it wasn't a whale but a Great White Shark*, you'd say—but for once, you were sleeping quietly. Your job at the new pot shop was wearing you out.

"Can anyone really live in a shark?" I thought drowsily.

Then the Casio was flashing 3:47 and a voice was peeping up from the blankets, urging me awake.

I sat alert, staring at the tapered gloom. Pressing my hand to the wall for balance, I tried not to wake you. But focusing on your warm skin, I found myself in a panic.

Earlier, we'd fought.

You're so full of shit your eyes are brown, I heard myself saying, a perennial favorite of my father's. I'd followed it with something ridiculous, light-headed, unhinged even. You hadn't responded. Was this why I'd stayed up so long, staring out? There was a new edge to everything, wasn't there?

"Gabriel?" I said.

"Let's begin," the voice insisted.

My bladder thickened. You continued to sleep, coma-like. I wriggled around you, clicked on the sound machine standby, "Gurgling Brook," and crept into the also sloping kitchen. The boards were old, shards of gone forests. The Famous Grouse was capless on the table where I'd left it.

"Leon," the voice said.

I stood there dimly and searched for its origin. In plain view was a giant mason jar of kombucha plus dividing mother. A pair of gunk-smeared garden gloves. An ancient *Vogue* with Tilda Swinton on the swanny-white cover.

"It's me!" the voice said.

The room smelled like snapped pine needles. In my chest, a river was bludgeoning heavy stones.

"Ms. Swinton?" I stammered.

Her alien parts and cinnamon hair, I'd always loved her, the queasy look she gave me!

But the voice came from somewhere closer, near my belly.

"You have a problem," the voice said.

I digested this halfway.

"I do?"

I thought hard. I pointed, finally, to the garden.

But our parasite disagreed.

"Do you know anything AT ALL," it said, *"about the history of Mexican art?"*

When I woke again, a belt of sun was cinching my eyes. Your bare torso moved around the kitchen, pouring maté water, stretching. Outside silent cars were starting up their phony, pre-recorded engines. *"Safety first!"* an automated voice announced.

I raised my head from my cardboard arms. I'd finished the night at the table with Tilda. Turning my cheek, I followed your movement. Your darker areolas met the fawn of your chest with the casual kismet of belonging. I suffered to join their easy glow.

"So that's it, I'm gone, blitzed, finally *cooked*," I said instead.
Your nostrils tightened.

"What happened."

"Gay bars are out!" I snapped my fingers to my thumb. I wanted to be back in your good graces but I resented working for it.

"Terry called," you said. "Did you really do something as substantially dumb as that?"

I sighed. My relationship to right and wrong had always been murky. I had a healthy, some said Catholic approach to guilt. But in recent years I'd begun to wonder if my guilt was so all-encompassing as to be irrelevant to any motive or consequence. The realization stranded me without a barometer. It was clear, I didn't trust myself with much. But I was also sure I could do no wrong. I toed every line almost religiously but was given to taking wild risks without any forethought at all, then, overcome with denial, hiding them.

"Gabriel," I said, *"Giga,"* throwing my arms toward your waist.

"I have to go," you said. *"Work."*

A new relationship was being drawn. You worked. I didn't.

I drifted around the apartment drinking expensive single-source coffee and clicking back and forth between Manhunt and my newest discovery, YardHard. The homepage was full of popups about "green bums" and "top tips for hoeing," but RAT574 seemed to know something.

Him: *Man knotweed is Axis of Evil numero uno. You got to be tenacious. Know how to spell that?*

Me: *You just did.*

Him: *Ok first let those suckers get big and hard. Then when they're dick thick ;) ;) ;) you machete off the tops RAMBO-style.*

Sun was banking off the window, showing all the grease on the thin glass.

Got me???

I twisted on my stool, staring at the yard's newest growths.

Got you.

Him: *Then you dump your kill juice down the stalk.*

Kill juice? It seemed extreme.

Me: *Can "kill juice" be organic?*

Him: *No way! Its got2be poison!*

Me: ...

Him: *Great band by the way.*

When I tried to remember why we'd fought, a gelatinous feeling descended. I was growing increasingly more wired from the caffeine plus somehow I was starving. The combo made me pharmaceutically woozy. Had our parasite, a microorganism who was leeching my precious nutrients, all those hard-earned dollars spent on kale and handpicked cashews, actually talked to me last night? Given me a lecture on art? I mean, there was Rivera of course, and Kahlo to be sure. But that was baby stuff. It was true, I knew next to nothing about Mexican art!

I depended on you to teach me things. Your father was a writer from the outskirts of Mexico City. Your mother was an engineer from Ottawa. You were the New North American: impervious—perfectly sealed off. That was why one night during our recent trip to Mexico, when we were refueling in central D.F., I wanted to go out alone. You were so chulo, so natural in the wide avenidas and plazas that nobody spoke to me and I was anxious to try out my Spanish.

"You stay here," I begged. We had taken over your friend's newly emptied Condesa apartment. "Go talk to your abuela or something."

Your father was her baby, which made you in every way preferential.

"On the telephone?" you said, rolling your eyes. "It's a big city, *maricón*."

"I don't know, eat flan then."

I was suddenly desperate to be alone.

"Grow up," you said. But instead of shoveling into your jacket you watched me go.

At noon it was time to take a Paradex from the naturopath. I grimaced and unscrewed the cap. Then I walked out into the yard. The season was changing. It would be light for hours and hours and hours. Pink shoots raved in the breeze, their heads glistening. They were much taller, already, since yesterday.

My feelings about objects had always been orphic—they penetrated my deepest levels. It was painful to be alive, I knew. Worse, I was somehow responsible. Undisturbed—walls, chairs, rocks, et cetera could fend for themselves. But my presence troubled the atmosphere. If, while walking, I kicked a rock but not the rock next to it, I created an imbalance, pointed at a wound. It then followed, *it was the rule*, that I turn around and similarly move the other rock. But what if I touched that second rock (it was bigger and so my toe needed more force to push it) longer than the first? Things were now severely out of whack.

"Sorry," I'd whisper, retracting my foot at hyper-speed.

Small crises like these followed me everywhere I went. Throwing out a dirty chopstick if its mate was clean made me pause at the trash can like an awful, disloyal god. Other times, lone discarded shoes or cracked bathroom tiles leered out to me. Don't notice them! I'd mutter. But their suffering was insistent.

Now my stomach gurgled but gave no further orders. Above me, a flight of molting pigeons swooped low. I juggled the pill anxiously. It was sweaty in my wintersoft palm. As if on auto-pilot, thinking about nothing, I used my thumb against the soil to dig a small indent. Then I plopped the dark gel cap in.

That night the clock dragged. You were late. I went to bed and kicked around. Our mattress felt like it was filled with over-turned traffic cones. For half an hour, I read about Rufino Tamayo. What, I began to wonder, did our parasite think of his 1978 work *La Gran Galaxia*? In it the figure, who wore some-thing like a jailbird's smock, was staring over a bowl of sea. As if a mirage, the inner pink organelle of his body was reflected out, shimmering over the blue expanse, while above the horizon line, a luminous geometry of constellations flexed.

The figure appeared to be yawning.

In quick succession, I sent you some texts.

One said: *Our parasite's kicking, is yours?*

No response. I continued.

I think I'm having contractions.

Silence. I switched tacks.

What's eating you? ;)

Tired of looking at an empty screen and the arrow that said *slide to unlock*, I turned off my phone.

I dreamed but my sleep was disturbed, watery. In it, I repeated a scene from my childhood. I had grown up near islands—rocky, fir-smothered pods on the north-northwest coast. As a kid I often accompanied my father in his boat.

One morning he woke me up early.

"There's been a wreck," he said.

We went down to Fidalgo Marina. Behind us, the sun simmered up over the Cascade range. The consensus among the boat owners was: Drunk Indians. There was a reef between the Lummi-owned Gooseberry Point and a local casino. During the night, a small Bayliner had hit it going full speed.

The men refilled their Styrofoam cups of coffee. Someone handed me one, topped to the brim. *Drunk Indians.* A no-brainer, everyone agreed. I was ten or eleven, newly effeminate. I liked to wear a solo rubber band in the back bud of my hair. I felt a chill and clutched my cup.

As the day went on, more news came in. There'd been six passengers, all still alive, but some were in pretty bad shape at Harborview and other trauma hospitals nearby. They'd been ejected forward from the boat, thrown like sacks onto the sharp rocks.

Toward evening my father let go of his usual German clamped lip. There weren't any deliveries to make. He could be wily, even impish at times. He closed the engine compartment where he'd been slowly tinkering at the fuel lines.

"Let's go," he said.

We untied and cut out across the strait. I struggled to nice up the buoys. I loved helping my father and did it with a silent pride. But I was brimming with the idea of the wreck. Violent pictures filled my mind. I found myself searching the waves for a sign of tragedy. In all directions, there was nothing. The afternoon was calm and hot.

Then the small tan boat tilted into sight. It lay halfway across the reef, which was, at low tide, a dwarf island.

My father cut the engine and brought in our bow.

"Go on," he said. "See what's in it."

I jumped onto the wreckage with a thud. Suddenly alone. I snooped as best I could. The category "Drunk Indians" dominated. I expected its presence to look fundamentally different from what my father and his brother did together with pails of Coors most nights. Fuck you, I muttered. Fuck you, fuck you. But here was no mess, no beer cans or incriminating plastic jug of booze. Just a small suitcase on the ripped-up fiberglass floor and the bracing zing of being this far away from land.

"Open it," my father pressed, his voice still close to me.

I hesitated. Drugs, I thought. Big plastic bags of coke powder like I'd seen on TV. My imagination was limited. *Money, Uzis.*

We were trespassing but my father had his own law.

Queasy, I unzipped the stiff fabric and looked down. A stack of clean washcloths crouched in the web of the opening, starched and tightly folded. I poked them. Towels, shirts. The bag was immaculately packed with someone's laundry, as if the person who owned it was going on a trip.

"Leon!" my father shouted.

The tide had flipped and the current was ripping sideways. Our bow dragged closer to the reef. We were a team; now he needed me. Dutifully, I hurdled aboard.

"What was it?" he said, as he slammed us into reverse. Freezing green water foamed over the transom.

"Nothing," I reported, facing ahead.

But that night I was stricken.

I'm sorry, I said again and again to my lowering bedroom ceiling. I'd done doubly wrong. I'd profited from someone else's bad time. But worse, what really concerned me, was that I'd left the bag abandoned with all that dark water surrounding it—the cloth open, its contents exposed.

I tried to tell you this once but you just shook your head.

"Your dad is nuts."

Now it was almost midnight and very hot. I thought about the small graveyard, a day's worth of pills, out in the yard. I fuddled with my phone's screen. A picture of your face flashed up when I touched your name. Your hair was short and your jaw was feral.

I paused.

Is this about Mexico? I jabbed down onto the screen.

In the D.F., having left you, I walked toward the park that I remembered marking the center of Condesa. Earlier in the day kids had been playing soccer on the concrete monument. Next to the fountain stood a series of columns whose plinths were covered in vines that evoked a jungly snarl without actually being unkempt. Together we'd sipped cans of Bohemia in the sun.

The entire trip, you'd been trying to show me something—at least, I thought you had. In front of me Parque México was blue and empty. I pulled another can of beer out from under my sweatshirt and sat with my back to a column's shaft. I wanted to go to Tropezedo—a club I'd read about in *El Mercurio*. Along the path that led out of the park, sodium lamps flashed on, popping and fuzzing into cold arcs. A figure moved between them with his head down. He seemed to be walking toward me, but without actually getting much closer or larger.

Watching him, I was furiously sad. We need separate, differentiated points, I realized, to understand the concept of space. The figure was of course you and the gap between us was only growing. No matter how hard you walked, you couldn't get to me. In between the lights, the shadows completely overtook you.

My palm was damp, wrapped around the can. I looked down, adjusting my grip. But when I raised my head again, the figure was suddenly directly in front of me. He wore Levis and black high-tops and his hair was long. How could I have thought he was you?

He paused, shifting from foot to foot. His breath was heavy from the effort.

"You want something?" he said in English.

"These are Megaspores," he grinned, uncapping his palm.

His fingers were smooth and his hands were big. Steam drifted from his body.

"No," I laughed, embarrassed.

Untroubled, he repeated himself and smiled again.

"These are Megaspores."

He crouched over me and slipped his hand into mine so now I was holding the mushrooms too. We stayed like that under the monument, touching.

Now I was pacing, far from sleep. I pushed into my jeans and a windbreaker; it was humid out and it seemed like it might rain. I descended into the subway. There was a stilled train that felt like a mirage of the train I needed to catch. *Lucky*. I loped on. Inside, the G was bright and yellow. It dragged through its dark funicular caverns and at Lorimer, the L platform was for once empty.

It's Friday night, I realized. I considered my options. The problem was, Terry was missing a case of top shelf. He thought I'd fenced it, used it at the BALLZDEEP party I occasionally threw. The accusation was lazy—easy to ignore. But the more I thought about the case I didn't steal, the more I realized how easy it would be to take.

To my left, the tunnel gaped sourly, waiting to spit out the next train.

"Don't you get it," I'd said to Gerald. We were adrift in the horizonless midpoint of a happy hour east of A.

"Between what I *might* do and what I *did* do—there's no difference at all!"

He stared at his brandy hand, planted thickly around his perpetual snifter.

"Have you ever eaten crêpes Suzette?" he said.

I knew by now that he'd cooked for Samuel, stubbornly brought him dishes at St. Vincent's even when Samuel was intubated, practically gone.

I spilled out for another round. "Yeah, yeah."

But he described the crêpes to me again in careful detail, so careful that even half-listening, I was sure I could smell them and taste them—the liqueury tangerine syrup, the brown crispness around the broken bubbles where the batter met the scorching, heavily buttered pan.

This train was taking forever.

"*Yo,*" interrupted a voice I recognized, sounding less like an art professor and more like an East Village court rat.

"*Yo, B-boy. You sure about this Tamayo cat?*"

I grabbed my gut. Was I sure about Tamayo? I mean, of course I should dig deeper, I had only just started to research.

"Shh!" I hissed into my windbreaker pouch.

But he was onstage now, looking for an audience.

My cheeks baked. It was my fault, I reasoned. Only I had stopped taking the pills—you were racing toward health. The more I thought about it the more it irked me. What was your rush? Let's convalesce together, baby, I wanted to shout. Yoga retreats, long raw food dinners—once we had planned to go to meditation on Tuesday nights.

I should get my own life!

I stared at the subway map of Manhattan. It had always looked like the profile of a big west-facing cock. Now a single beam glared out from the tunnel. I watched as it grew bigger and bigger to the point of engulfing me—then suddenly sliced into two.

* * *

I emerged through the mechanized subway door at First Avenue limp-legged. Under my windbreaker, my T-shirt was sweat-logged and I wrung the left corner of it until my fingers made prints in the cotton. The rest of me was wiry but no matter how many pull-ups I did my chest was soft. The wet fabric pooled there expectantly.

I slid through the turnstile cage with my head down. The message I'd sent you drifted in space without defense. I jammed my phone from my pocket, waiting for the signal to show.

It had rained while I'd been underground, and a tuberous smell came up from the pavement. I wiped my face, finally street-level. In this early-summer heat and quickly hosed sky, thousands of safety bulbs speckled the half-built condos: mutant-sized fireflies.

I no longer felt capable of being out. Shapes walked around in the dark with their shoulders bunched. I checked my phone again: blank. Mindlessly I logged onto YardHard as I moved. Rat574 ballooned up—he was perpetually "in the garden."

Me: *nice night.*

Him: *want to score?*

I'd followed Megaspores toward what I guessed was Avenida Michoacán, trailing at a distance. Lebanese cypress lined the path, shooting upward, roughly rimmed by giant palm fronds. He walked briskly. I'd entered an alternate universe and was meeting an unknown version of myself who could have easily starred in *Cruising*.

Branches stretched over us like arms. Stuffed in my pocket, my left hand prickled where he'd held me. He walked faster, taking a staircase two at a time toward the corner of the park. His hips were narrow. Exposed, they'd be sharp. Yours are like that too and when you let me, I grabbed them as if you were a view scope and I was trying to stare inside. I imagined you back at the apartment moving around with purpose, turning the pages of a book or licking a joint.

At the top of the stairs, there was a small plaza. Megaspores stopped. We stood there, again very near. His long hair was oiled, glimmering in the light. Around us the atmosphere of the city buzzed and blared. I tipped the rest of my beer down my throat.

"Duck pond," he said, pointing to our left. Helpless, my eyes followed. Where the concrete broke off, there was a low patch of water and, I supposed, a fountain. Then he grinned again and under the sodium lamp I could see the 'shroom caps hiding between his gums and teeth—he'd been chewing and chewing as we walked.

"Duck pond," I repeated lamely.

Then I was mashing my lips against his open mouth, running my tongue everywhere. Duck pond, I thought again. His saliva was casting a kind of spell. Now my mouth was full of wet brown caps. *Duck pond*, my brain insisted. The substance was leathery, crumbly, and underneath, fecal, soft.

I shoved him against the cement base of the lamppost. He was my same height exactly. I felt his hips warm and springy on mine. But this had nothing to do with him! I was only finishing an act of balancing that he'd started when we asymmetrically touched. Meanwhile my cheeks had begun to fizz. I felt full of goop and light. I saw you at the balcony window waving. You and I hated each other sometimes but together we'd be fine.

"Tentigo." Megaspores pointed, laughing.

I shrugged off my hard-on. *So what?* But I was becoming confused about which parts of me had touched him and which hadn't. That morning in the shower you'd bent down wide for me to fuck you but I couldn't relax and you'd turned off the water with your hair full of soap.

Now my upper lip was coated in sweat but when I ran my tongue along it the hairs were sour. He moved farther away. My brain was whirring. He must know Tropezedo, I thought. Light pooled around him in bright beams. My nipples pulsed where his chest had been. The distance was suddenly constant: unbearable. I closed the space with my arms but as if disconnected from my brain my hands crashed into his denim-covered ribs and crotch and then whacked at his chest.

"I'm hitting you," I heard my voice saying.

I sounded hysterical.

"ESTOY fucking *PERFORADO.*"

He sidestepped me easily, dropping to the ground in a kind of squat thrust. Then he put his face down into the weeds. Beyond my panting I heard cars and sirens parading the boulevards. Blandly, as if he were at the clinic about to get a booster shot, he inched his jeans over his chonie-less ass.

"I'm Carlos," he said, turning his misty head to me.

I passed through the Friday night party tents and teepees of the East Village in a hurry. This season everyone was tall and leafy. A girl with flaming hair smoked under the spastic yellow of Gray's Papaya. Tilda again. She was like you. Safe from pain—emotionally no holes at all.

At the corner of C and Tenth, I bent over. All those pills in the dirt, now my bowels were involved. The leftover vegetarian gumbo I'd geniusly eaten for dinner slushed back and forth. I concentrated on squeezing my ass closed. Any port in a storm, I thought, whimpering my body through the fudge-colored door of the Baltic.

I stared around the familiar scape. Behind the long run of oak laminate, the cracked stools, the bartender's skin emitted a neon sparkle. The new guy was just Terry's type, as twinky as they come.

"Hey," I said.

"Uh-huh."

He swished his towel over a chalky spot I'd scrubbed a thousand times before.

"I need the staff bathroom," I said. "I work for Terry. I run, you know..."

Wincing, I paused, giving him the chance to make something up.

"Uh-huh."

"Give me the keys." I stretched out my palm. "Right?"

"I should call Terry."

Casually I rejoined a stray straw to its holder.

"You could," I said. "In this shitty economy where no one trusts anyone, it's one of those things you could do."

I was yelling, the Baltic had become ear-splitting. Out near the dance floor and the wall gallery of second-rate reindeer heads, a karaoke machine blared. Someone was murdering Meatloaf. A guy with a bristly beard stood up on a chair and waved his arms. *I would do anything for love!* he shouted.

The bartender shrugged. His eyebrows said: I'm hot?

Fields of Japanese knotweed plowed through my brain. I caught myself in the long barroom mirror. My eyes looked like meatballs. I thought suddenly of RAT574. What a guy, he really cared . . . thick-chested, chest hair glistening, a warrior with Teutonic strength blasting our personal scourge from the face of Brooklyn eternal.

Would it really be so bad to have a clean yard? I saw us sitting there in it, drinking icy things. Weeds are like hair on the body of the earth, I said to myself. *Not personal.*

My pocket buzzed. I took a deep breath. One message.

Slide, *yes.*

The text bubble popped. I squinted down.

Mexico??? you said.

I took the master key ring and made off into the annals of the bar with my heart wacking. Past the urinals, the pool table, the broken-off pay phone and its Sharpie forest. I had no idea what I was doing, only that Terry owed me my last check. I stood in the small liquor-barricaded office. Hundred-dollar scotches stared me down.

I wanted to know. Had you taken Terry's side? When it came down to it? Or did you believe me?

It was dawn when I got to the Condesa apartment and the fruit vendors were unlocking their carts. I slid under the crisp sheet.

"How was Tropezedo?" you said, petting my abdomen. "Same old pinochas?"

I nodded.

But Tropezedo had been black and shiny, practically Scandinavian, packed with Carlos's friends and bowls of metallic condoms sitting everywhere like grapes. Then there was Cockspot and a series of other bars with similar names. Over the course of the night my body had become big and dim and I floated in it like a visitor.

The next morning, we left for Oaxaca on a small seven-seater plane. I sat next to the pilot, a gaucho in polished aviators. As we skidded over the dark green hilltops, my hands crept under the backs of my heat-pancaked thighs. My head was in a tequila-made vise. With the copilot's controls in front of me, I was sure I was about to wrench the plane down into the jungle floor.

Later, at the airport cafeteria, you were ebullient.

"Did you see it?"

My face was gray. *"Giga,"* I confessed, staring at your beautifully remote nail beds.

You grabbed my shoulders as if I was made of rocks.

"Earth to Leon," you said, cradling my head, laughing. "We landed, we're *safe.*"

A sick feeling spooled inside me. My vision turned to pixels and points. Our parasite rammed my sphincter. And my sphincter was just a weak wall! I could crawl to the bathroom but for what? For once I was exactly where I needed to be. Sweating, I unbuckled my belt and crouched down. Hanging my ass back past my heels, I squatted wider, my ankles pitching forward. This would disgust you. "Raunch factor ten," you'd say. But what about Herrera, Bustamante, and No Grupo? Our parasite and I—we were careening toward a more conceptual kind of art.

I palmed the cash shelf for balance, breathing with yogic purity. The carpet smelled of large cat. Forget about order. I opened and a sheet of water and rice poured out, then I was sure I felt something tug free from my stomach lining and whoop down the chute. I stared between my legs—I felt suddenly better than I had in months. *Out out!* I chanted. In this zen state I could finally give as much as I wanted and more would come gushing down to fill the void always.

My phone rang.

I wiped with a discarded bar rag and quickly stood up.

"Hello?" RAT574 said. He sounded different than I'd expected, breathless and old, like he'd been sitting for too long with something in his hand.

I eased the office door closed and gave it a quick twist. The Baltic was blurry, more crowded. "Leon!" Gerald called from his appointed stool, but I barely recognized him. I threw the keys in the direction of the bar and ducked out into the cooling night, shoving the curtain out of my way.

At Fourteenth Street, a wad of guys with gym hats padded past plus all the regular queens but this time they must have been joking, their makeup caked thick and droopy.

I dropped down into the First Avenue subway.

Drunks plastered the lavender seats. A Poetry in Motion poem attacked my eyes, then an ad for Botox. Halfway through the tunnel I slammed a cartoon hand onto my forehead: you were in Chinatown at your brother's, a plan you'd made weeks ago, probably under a roll-neck of Xbox and bong smoke.

It didn't matter, I told myself. In Terry's office I'd remembered my only rule. This rule trumped all others, which perfectly explained the crumpled shape of my life. As a kid I had another habit. Whenever something was too ruined, too bereft, or sick— say a saucer with no matching cup, a napkin mostly unused but with a splotchy stain, a baby mole tugged half-dead by a dog—I crushed it. More than anything I couldn't stand to see suffering.

"Giga," I said into your voice mail, as I stood on our corner of McGuinness and Nassau, waiting for who knows what.

I took a breath.

Then I confessed all kinds of things into the flat receiver— disgusting attachments, lies blotting back as far as I could see, betrayal upon teetering betrayal—anything and everything that ran into my mind.

Can You Live with It

"So Raskolnikov goes to Siberia and that's supposed to be it—he's absolved, a big flat vacant plane," I hear myself saying.

"Yeah?" We drink from our beer cups and look at the waves.

"Actually," I say, "he has to work all of this hard labor and what's-her-name visits him every day so piously and the other inmates hate him until finally, he cries on a riverbank: 'I'm here! *Alive*, inescapably part of things.'"

Or something.

But Siberia's nothing like Alcatraz, how it's just sitting out here in the middle. The bay and surrounding hills all drought-brown. We're on one of those SF boats watching a dissipated Marin dude hit on women and slaughter Willie Nelson songs while the sun does its thing as advertised by Blue and Gold

Bay Cruises or maybe it's the Red and White; we go on those too whenever I come from New York back to town.

We tip him then feel like jerks instantly. Our beer fund lost in an oversized cowboy boot that's sitting in front of his guitar case like: "I just took this off for you." Except the boot is huge and he's wearing sneakers.

"That was stupid," my buddy says, pulling her lips so her cheeks bump her eyes and her gums glare.

"We can't just pull it back out?" I say.

Now we're standing at the onboard bar with its wood grain laminate drinking free water. Slug after slug in plastic cups. Or belt after belt, whatever our alcoholic progenitors called it.

"This tastes like butts."

"But you can live with it," assures the bartender. She's got on a bow tie and the Glade green Christmas lights under her shirt make her breasts glow lopsidedly. She turns the key on the little gate that holds the booze in place. We hear it lock.

Then there was that long night Raskolnikov spent on the bridge over the Neva. The cash-it-all-in night. The one where he's thinking: *Am I too bad.*

And doesn't his mother come?

This morning I walked up and down Folsom Street. It was foggy and damp. Then I sat in the linoleum-floored waiting room, identical to a mall DMV except for the FREE HIV TEST SITE and posters of sexually transmitted cartoony bugs taped all over the walls. The digital clock had those requisite cement fingers. I rubbed my number's paper dart against my jeans.

In the tiny examination room the clinician gave me a folding chair. "This is going to get real personal," she said.

"Sure thing," I said. "Uh-huh."

From the interior cabin of the Blue and Gold we watch the sun finishing up. The windows are black. There's a buffet table full of clammy ham wedges and crudités. We climb the narrow carpeted stairs just in time to hear the cowboy deliver his final pitch:

"If I said you had a great body, would you hold it against me?"

It's just us and two Taiwanese newlyweds on their honeymoon staring toward what was, only minutes ago, the Rock.

"So you're telling me he walked around with an ax in his sack? Then hacked an old lady just to see if he could?"

"Pretty much," I say.

"Sorry," my buddy says to the cowboy. She reaches her arm back down into the boot's funnel.

More shots.

But somehow we've docked and we're moving back down the stairs and the little bar light with the red plastic face is out and the plastic cups are being rushed to their plastic bag.

We disembark. Another bar. Streamers hang from the ceiling in crumbly garlands. We bail out bills from a battered ATM. Two beers, two Cazadores. We're talking about my ex-girlfriend and "how bad it was."

"It's like it was genetically impossible for you to realize how bad it was."

"Yeah, I know," I say.

I concentrate on the curdled smell that hovers cadaverously whenever a bar's been sucked at for years. Back then I was a wreck. Practically immolating humans with dicks for dicking.

"But why *didn't* you?"

"What?" I say.

Now my buddy gets a phone call or a text, I forget which, from *her* ex-girlfriend who used to strip in North Beach. We go outside. My buddy has that smile glued on. She towers over six feet tall, Irish-cum-Viking.

Cabs! We stand on the street with that nebulas-instead-of-neurons tequila feeling.

"Mind if we?"

"You look okay," the cabbie says hopefully.

We take the back roads over Telegraph Hill. The cab's a relic, it swallows the street. I hold my breath, bunch my rib cage and underneath, what my Pilates teacher calls, "my meat." Suddenly we're blinking at Coit Tower and there's the Golden Gate again all lit up, now too far to touch.

"Do you do intravenous drugs," the clinician said, swiping her lips and capping her ChapStick.

"Do you have multiple partners, do you fuck men, what about bi guys, you know, bisexuals, do you practice *no glove no love*?"

She pushed up her glasses, attendant. How was the dusty overhead so fluorescent? My armpit hair forming small damp pads.

Are you and your partner "trying out new things," do you take it raw, do you cumdump.com, do you or does anyone you know suck bagfuls of strange as in weird dick?

Couldn't I just give her something to write down, join the world, say yes?

"I'm sorry," she said, doing another circuit with the Chap-Stick then looking at her watch. "You don't qualify for a test. It's cost versus probability. You're just not at risk."

"Huh?" I said.

It was cousin to that feeling I'd had when my friend and a girl he liked had been too deep in each other to do anything but fuck condomless on the floor and she'd gotten instantly pregnant. Instantly pregnant—was there any other way? Hearing the story I knew I should have been relieved. I would never inject semen against the fecund walls of someone's receptive cavity and bam! make a squirmy life someone would then have to abort or love or, worse and infinitely sadder, both.

I squinted back at the fluorescent.

"For anything?" I'd said to the clinician.

"Not as we see it," she said.

We stand at the next bar, inside the "Hungry I." My face is hot from the neck up, as if red construction paper has been stapled to my cheeks and throat. The sign above the bar is big and bulby with lights. A large Egyptian-style eye glows on the surface of the sign, the eye all-knowing somewhere in the heavy black strokes of the iris, its gaze clamping me down. The neon letters keep rearranging: *I Hungry I Hungry I Hungry.*

"Is she coming?" I ask.

We've used this excuse before to end up exactly here, so we know how it goes.

"No."

We enter the half-moon of the stripper pit. Each dancer gets three songs. The first is a warm-up, the second is more athletic, kind of a talent showcase, the third is the real deal, the song *she* picks. Songs like Rihanna, "Pour It Up."

In the video the hem of Rihanna's fur coat is soaking, the light a murky green. She drags the fur onto a throne.

"They're all lesbians, right," I say.

I know this to be true. When I lived here my friends worked at the Lusty Lady and the Hustler Club and they were lesbians.

I would never have used that word in those days. I'd tortured myself with it as a kid. Invoking it like a mantra inside the privacy of my skull, hoping I would gag each time the word appeared or, better, because it was more extreme and therefore more convincing, actually puke. But now that I lived in New York somehow the word was okay. Upcycled even; everyone used it. My girlfriend said it, my girlfriend fucked men, even if my girlfriend fucked men and then fucked me and didn't tell me about it I still was not at risk, I was that safe. I was a lesbian.

The stage is industrially clean. Men sit in wads along the arc, holding large glasses of something vodka-like. The lights glare purple then black then purple again. My buddy leans in.

Whenever we are in strip clubs like these we put our shoulders up and wear the physiognomy of underdeveloped teenage boys.

These clubs have become kind of an issue. Lately we've been meeting in Vegas or Atlantic City—or she visits me in New York. Then we go to exotic rooms of the worst kind: Pumps, Sugardaddy's. Even in metropolitan Queens there'll be oversized trucks parked outside with pit bulls in the back of them—chunky sad dogs whose black leather harnesses are covered in spiked metal cones, their owners lubricating themselves from plastic cups, bare-chested, muscles slathered on in the droopy four p.m. light.

It's similar to the way we once did drugs. A boundary existed, we put ourselves near it magnetically. If someone offered shots we'd dump half out; if someone palmed us a tiny plastic bag we'd smile, pound their shoulders *no thanks*, thrilled for them that they were on the road to a good time. Then somewhere in the ditch between the beginning of the night and last call, the "no" would shift positions. We weren't interested in judging or withholding from those around us—we were good people with capacious lives, if we had to spend the next five hours locked in a bar blowing cheap Outer Mission coke with so-and-so to make them feel more human, we could do it, we had that to give.

In the morning we'd lurch awake, sweatily call each other: *we felt fine!* Agree that despite so-and-so's oversensitivity and those few last shots everything had been tidy and right: bar inventory overstocked, the doors locked—chain and padlock and gate with photo on phone to prove it—all okay, presentable, all good.

"I'm still trying to understand," said the clinician. "Let's give it one more try. Why *exactly* are you here?"

I reapproach the bar, give a too-big smile, feel a kind of cool blade of exposure when the bartender looks at me. I'm not sure what I want except for her to see me entirely, which I hope means myself but also, somehow better. *"Two beers, two Cazadores."*

"We only have Jose Cuervo," she says.

I seem to have large clumps of cash jammed in all of my pockets. A phone.

I fumble with it. Texts everywhere, eight or nine of them.

I shove it in my jeans, beams of diffuse meaning pouring at her from the backs of my eyes.

In the bathroom my face is pale. Exudes a kind of drippy pouch-like quality. The toilets are empty, still I rehearse at the mirror:

Big smile. *Where else should I pee? The bar floor?*

Outside, I stare through the drizzly crinkle at Columbus Avenue and North Beach. A few guys trolling the corner bodega. Two bouncers insulating the door with their woolen coats. Even before Siberia, the whole book is sweaty and freezing. Like when Raskolnikov spends three days jammed up under one measly blanket, his teeth jackhammering. Of course his body had caught *something*—but didn't even know what it had caught???

I scroll through the texts.

Baby it wasn't a thing.

When you act like this it makes me WANT to fuck other people.

I can hear the curated hip-hop where she must be, the jizz-sprayed booth of some Chinatown/L.E.S. club like Jing Fong, the complete shittiness of it all.

It's like you're in your own stupid world?

Back inside, my buddy is in the same place, same smile. I slide into the seat beside her. The dancer we unanimously think is hot—by which we mean the girl who we think understands us—is on the pole mid-routine. Her legs are muscly, tattooed with black roses. Six-inch heels.

"How's it going," I say to my buddy.

I see a small bale of ones in front of her. Whenever men are near us we try to outspend them, peeling cash from every financial obligation, our rent, car insurance, whatever, all of it, dumping each bill shyly down.

"I'm not sure I can come to New York," she says.

"What?" I say over the blasting speakers. This next trip was going to be an Atlantic City plus NYC extravaganza, a ridiculous double feature.

"It's just getting kind of . . . you know?"

I try to smooth the mass of dollars from my pocket. The dancer bends over the gap where the stage ends, slowly miming an upside-down over-the-pants dick suck to a disease-riddled Governor Christie–looking dude. She comes our way. I adjust my lap. Work to meet her eyes. Take a breath, look at my crotch, think: mound instead of hole.

We're sharing some kind of trembling second. I know it's stupid to believe this but I do. It says something like *life is excruciating* but says it prismatically—holding the completeness and incompleteness both. Then, when she's nearest to me, with the lights zapping her nipples and everything gorgeous and breathless between us, she balks, veers back to the pole.

"What the fuck?" my buddy mouths, pouring out more ones.

"I can't even fucking get AIDS," I say. "Can you believe that?"

My lesbian friend who danced at the Lusty Lady liked to meet us in the bar after work. She was always chipper, always the same. The night had been great, she'd made $$$ money, of course there were ASSHOLES but there were assholes everywhere, on BART, at the Laundromat, men gumming up the street touching you whenever you walked by.

We'd laugh about it, it was funny, hysterical even.

Then there was that time in the swimming pool. Her eyes fixed on us from the bottom.

My hands are clammy. Back up at the bar: *"Two Cazadores."*

"I told you before, we only have Cuervo."

In *Crime and Punishment* it wasn't the real Neva he was standing over that night, anyway, it was just the Obvodny Canal, the city's sewer.

"Can you deal?" the bartender wants to know. "Sweetie?"

I'm nodding up and down. *But doesn't his mother come? But doesn't his mother come?*

Containers

EVERYONE WANTED TO GO TO PATES ET TRADITIONS LIKE usual. It was de facto becoming the only place we hung out. "It's *et* not *and!*" I was always being told, like currently, by Jim, at the L train's exit.

"Nah," I said, begging off. I was getting a pate gut. Then it was only Pilates Pilates Pilates, Pilates for days. At night I breathed the Reformer. In the morning I breathed ujjayi-style like Darth Vader. But the stubborn water wing around my belly wouldn't deflate.

"Suit yourself," said Jim. "It's Monday, I wouldn't miss the carrot pate."

Instead I called my dealer. "What're you doing?" I said.

"Umm, is this rhetorical?" she said. I shrugged. Tiny spring goose bumps were running up and down my arms.

"Where are you?" I continued. I stared at an icy clump that had a stroller sticking out of it and by this point in the season was never ever going away.

"Why are you breathing like Darth Vader?" she said. "I'm at Pates et Traditions with everyone, come over."

At length, I said I would.

She laid the product out next to the pate boards.

"Get that one," said Jim. He poked a Captain Caveman-looking bud with a paint-spotted finger.

"Martha Stewart, good choice," my dealer said. She put some orange goo on a fork.

"Martha Stewart?" I said. "What happened to, like, Strawberry Kush?"

"Martha Stewart's actually a huge pot activist," my dealer said. "I can't believe *you* of all people don't know that."

"Yeah," said Jim, eyebrowing me incredulously. "M. Diddy! She radicalized in jail."

In New York, when spring finally comes, you atomize. Your sense of containment, a survival mechanism in winter, dislodges, melts. At least, this is what I thought as I walked down North Sixth. I was sad, but the sadness had a wet, loose quality that broke my chest apart as I inhaled the weed. I stepped between the sidewalk's gray meringues and stubborn plow-made bergs. *And Traditions? Et Traditions?*

Under my down parka, new scars wrinkled from each armpit to sternum. Their ley lines red and tight.

I'm worried once you do it, I won't be attracted to you anymore.

I mean what if I'm not?

I mean, what if?

I approached the river. A wind gurgled up. I breathed deep and sith-y. *Luke, I'm your father.* Was that what he'd said? I'd never actually seen any *Star Wars* movies. It was one of a vast number of childhood shames. But I did know that the moment had something to do with encountering the dark side. Now I heard a strange whistle coming out of the back of my throat, or near it.

"M. Diddy," I said. Sure enough, she was whistling. Her platinum-ness enveloped.

We stared at the old Domino Sugar factory. Battered excavators, banana yellow. A traffic-smeared bridge.

"You can't unboil an egg," she said.

"It's really good pot," I wanted to tell her.

Beside Myself

UNDER THE SHEETS I WAS BESIDE MYSELF. EVERY WAY I turned, I was there. It was hot twisted up in my IKEA Cal king. Desert towns like Flamingo Heights and Morongo sprawled beyond my windows darkly. I'd been drinking beer again, despite the new study saying hops are full of estrogen. They'd snuck it in somehow. The micro-brews, IPAs, and "hop-ocalypses" were even worse. I touched above my scars. Was the tissue regrowing?

Flax, hemp, soy all had it too. Back in LA my girlfriend knew this—too much estrogen made it hard to have a baby. I swayed at the bathroom's doorway. She was two hours east. Hard to have a baby, together or apart.

In bed again, I spent some time Instagramming, reviewing my follow requests. Every name *almost* 100 percent familiar. I'd narrow in on an image. Can't. Trying in the shock of blue light to sleuth out whose Tecate can had just been tossed onto

which gallery floor, whose taste in succulents evinced real sensitivity, whose carefully composed meals were being held out for
my approval. *Was that who? Wasn't that? No. Yes?* I didn't know.
Casualness was key. Better to let them sit on the dock unac-
cepted but also unrejected.

I pulled over a desert mag from the bedside table. I was
halfway into an article on the Mojave green rattlesnake. They
had a neurotoxin most snakes did not. More armed, they main-
tained powerful enemies. The king snakes and milk snakes,
namely, what the article called "other royalty."

Other royalty also bothered me. In junior high my best
friend and I had performed a less-than-consensual role-play.
The friend was Queen Elizabeth. I, more flawed so more pas-
sionate, was Mary, Queen of Scots. We dropped daggers
through the grates in each other's lockers. "Mary." "My Dear
Elizabeth," the notes read. The fight was about loyalty. How
my body had sworn allegiance to something fatally perverted—
gym-teacher-like—which everyone knew permanently con-
signed me to the two-way mirrors in the locker room, stuck
with whoever was also sitting behind them, eating microwaved
food and looking.

"My Dearest Mary."

"Elizabeth."

Living on borrowed time, I took solace knowing Mary's
dogs poured out from under her skirt, biting her executioner
after her head rolled.

Outside it was mute for miles. I reached up and adjusted the
bedside lamp. To protect themselves, Mojave rattlesnakes performed something called "body bridging." Hiding their heads,

they rose up from the sand in flat racket-like loops. Now each snake became larger, morphing into multiple bodies or a new composite body—made up entirely of obfuscating bends. Refusing to be consumed, each snake-self produced another, more terrifying self. I flung the magazine and turned off the light, at ease.

Drift in a new place long enough and you no longer feel your adopted world in such sharp, euphoric relief. That abandoned pinky-hued cinder block shack whose emptiness, a few days ago, was so significant? I no longer saw it, I let it enter me: we were joined. Everywhere boundaries blurred as if from out of the windows of a moving car. I was always driving anyway. Covering great distances, speeding from place to place.

There were more sex offenders in the desert than anywhere else. Everyone knew this, apparently, the same way everyone knew about the ubiquitous marines and hippies who covered the landscape or popped up from what seemed like surprising holes against the otherwise lunar flat. Was it a universe-made law—some bodies needed more space? The thought returned to me as, on a morning trip to Sky Village Swap Meet, I swerved over for a couple huddling against a scraggy creosote tree.

"Hi," I said, zipping down the window, feeling the air-conditioning rush away.

"We're coming from the dentist," she said. "They unscrewed four of his teeth."

She gestured to a wrinkled paper bag he, in an outsized Lakers jersey and oily jeans, was clutching. There was no town in any direction, at least not for miles and miles.

They couldn't be dangerous because *she* was there. Or was it, I was not ever in danger? No one looked at me with letchy thoughts. No one tried to touch me in the grocery line at the Vons. I wasn't given things, or not given things, because of my attention-soliciting bulges. I twisted the radio back to full decibels. There was a female component in every equation that either made things safer or less safe.

"We're from Texas," she shouted over the blare. They dutifully climbed into the back, preserving the passenger seat, I noticed, for the other me.

He nodded. "Never seen the desert! Or the mountains. Came for a funeral and just stayed!"

I surveilled the hazy glow of the road ahead. Part of him was in a bag and the rest of him was also contained by something, now my car and the white Mojave heat writhing across the jagged valley I'd likewise crammed myself into two weeks ago.

"Where to?" I shouted, gunning ahead. Newspaper headlines, six p.m. TV reports like: "Sickos masquerading as 'a couple from Texas' . . ." suddenly mixed with the throb of the stereo. Out here I listened exclusively to dance music, it was the only thing big enough.

Never seen the mountains? Never seen a desert? I fastened them with the rearview. What if the funeral hadn't happened yet?

Because the death hadn't happened yet?

"Pull over here," the woman said, perhaps sensing my edginess.

I reclamped the wheel, we were in sight of the Valero anyway. She unbuttoned her lock. But the bag bugged me.

"Open up!" I said, craning my neck as they got out.

He shrugged and held it to me. The contents were a raw red color, having just been wrenched from his mouth.

Sky Village Swap Meet was behind the Yucca Valley Arco station; you turned into it from Old Woman Springs Road. Old Woman Screams, I always said in my head, but now I didn't notice it, just made the matter-of-fact substitution. Old women did scream.

I parked.

Recently I'd been gripped with a phobia about places. It seemed to me that places were inevitably marked by their future potential. I was at Sky Village Swap Meet now. But I might also be here again. And who knew under what conditions?

I wound in among the stalls of rugs and chipped ceramics, crunched hats. This future visit scratched, waiting to humiliate me. Being beside myself made it harder. As if I were twinning and the twin of me twinning and them too, twinning again.

In LA I was trying to get my girlfriend pregnant with my brother's sperm but his sperm had a morphological quirk that meant it wouldn't enter the egg. Each time we tried it was beautiful, portent with signs—I woke in the middle of the night in the grip of huge white birds, I heard voices, somewhere fatherhood had started. Then nothing. This produced a rage so deep I thought I'd never be free of it, until the next month, when I begged that we try again.

I loved those aberrant microscopic shapes. Given the chance, I knew they could do things others couldn't. Plus they seemed to prove, even more definitively than the fact I'd seen him emerge grayly from our shared mother, my brother was related to me. There was something in our mutual code that refused the dictate *form as function*. He was related to me; my nonworking body set the terms, enforced the relation. He'd always been mine—my responsibility, above all, not to hurt. But had my coming out so misfitting like this, years ahead, *already* hurt him?

I touched a stain-blotched blanket.

"Fifty bucks."

The vendor, tanned, black cheek-scruff, was hot and loose. *Fuselage*, I felt, staring. I wanted to be that way. Could I, also as fuselage, jerk him off behind the dingy bathroom block, hold his junk in my palm, drive the 10 West one-handed whispering procreation songs?

I'd arrive. His sperm would shuttle through my psyche, exit my invented spigot. It had to be okay, we were on a biological deadline. Time, in this regard, was panting.

Not mine, drilled my body.

But my hand remained on the blanket. The heat made me cloudy. My fingers had the sensitivity of toilet paper rolls. *Fuselage* was thick, it left a greasy skid. Didn't it just mean body?

"Fifty," he said again. His ears (too small) broadcasted an overabundant relationship to control, a not-so-secret anal vibe. My brother's ears were nice, open, large. He was a DJ. I smiled grittily, moved on.

How was it then that the other me, now completely rogue, was nodding *yes* as the vendor explained the blanket had been his dead mother's, was an heirloom, maybe even turn-of-the-century Navajo—moreover that he was about to call it quits, was packing up, I was his last customer?

"Here's sixty," that other me said, waving away the change. I jammed the blanket into a too-small plastic grocery bag.

Encouraged, he dug out an Altoids box from his jeans pocket.

"Ever seen a rough diamond?"

I paused. Did diamonds in the rough actually exist?! I could only picture the shape described—in fact, defined—by "diamond."

I bent in, coughing from peppermint dust. The tin was full of splintered safety glass.

"Windshield," he admitted, carefully repocketing them.

The vendor rows fed into a central plaza. To my left: Sky Village concession. Straight ahead, what the red arrows (staked every-where) had been announcing: Bob's Crystal Cave. From what I could tell, it was a slumpy dome made of spray foam.

The blanket would be good, I thought. My girlfriend would like it if she visited. And she had to visit; we had things to dis-cuss. But lately I hadn't felt like talking. A sharp-edged disc would bob in my throat, would swell into a wet gushy sack—*I'd swallowed a water wienie*—how were we ever going to make a baby? Leaning from the noon sun into the sheltered overhang between the bathrooms and the Crystal Cave, tears clustered up, I was crying.

A voice from my side:

"Would you like to see my joy?"

Must be Bob, I guessed. White ZZ Top beard, prospector's garb. His mouth cranked to "smiling." He had a joy, the other me wanted him to feel good about it. I adjusted my hat so I could wipe my eyes unnoticed.

"Okay," I said.

Pressing flat my freshly made chest, I balanced by making my voice higher: less threatening.

"I'm beside myself," I said, gesturing at what was evident.

"This is my second cave," Bob said, ignoring us. "When they tried to take Sky Village from me I smashed the first one to pieces."

We navigated the darkness of the entrance. Slathered with polyurethane, it had the atmosphere of a mine shaft that brown strings of party goo had exploded over. I kicked—snake patrol— into hot black space.

"I put everything I have into her," he whispered, pushing me through a small doorway in the cave's hump-like frame. He stayed outside, his grip tight. "I'll lock her so no one else can get in."

His joy, his joy. The door clicked. I kept myself from jiggling it. I wanted Bob to feel the force of my support. I breathed the aquarium air. This was a trust act. But regarding the Astro-Turf, the chemically nonliving smell, the amethysts glued in every direction across the floor that also contained miniature diorama-style lakes, glades, rivers (made similarly of sad shiny crystals)—I began to sweat. *Some bodies needed more space.* When I stretched my arms they touched each other in mirror effect, then touched the all-too-cavelike sides.

I shoved back against the small platform bench. A Plexiglas porthole discharged daylight at the crystals but sitting under it, where the bench was, no one could see me. Leaning over, I tested the door. Stiff and unyielding. Was this where he put them? *The kids?* A sex offender. It couldn't be more clear. Dude was an abuser—the worst kind of felon—hiding out there near the Disco Dogs and Agave Slush, in plain sight.

Toch.

I'd recently changed my text notification. The sound now a wooden mallet banging a hollow nut. It was my brother. Just his name and my eyes swam wetly.

I'm locked in Bob's Crystal Cave, I texted back.

What??? [alien emoji]???, he typed.

I know, I said.

Then followed it (I couldn't help myself) with my usual, all the phallic signs—the eggplants and bananas and corncobs, the lollipops, cactus, and volcanoes. I was older, was supposed to be the one helping him, but these days the dam had exploded, I couldn't stop asking him for everything.

Is anyone with you?, he said. *Sister?*

I glanced in front of me at the crystal river. Water flowed down but it seemed sulfurous, "off." I hated the smell. I was sure nothing was living here, the crystals least of all. Sperm, on the other hand, were tough—had an epic life span, could swim for days. Moreover, in any given ejaculation, each of the millions of tadpoles had been growing for an entire three months, doing what I couldn't do. Becoming.

"Baby, are you there?"

I sat up, unflattening a minuscule forest. My legs felt sodden.

My girlfriend, who'd been in LA all morning, was outside the Crystal Cave. Her jade eyes, her voice. Wasn't there another word? *Jadite*? Green. Impressed, someone had recently told her that.

"Yeah."

I thought they were jade too but had always been too embarrassed to say it.

"Hi," she said.

"You're here." I rubbed my arm where a finger-shaped bruise was surfacing.

"Ummm some guy Bob," she said, "he's at the med tent asking for Band-Aids."

Good! I thought. I imagined horrified fathers or raging mothers with baseball bats.

"Your brother called." Her voice was muted by the foam. "Baby? You've been in there for hours?"

A Disco Dogs wrapper and two wadded cans of Pepsi lay on the patch of floor, on top of the blanket I had apparently unrolled.

"Do you think you might want to come out?"

Had that been me, some hours earlier, rejogging the door? The lock was swollen but it opened. Then exiting into the brutal heat of the afternoon. I'd stretched—*free!*

Bob—founder of Sky Village Swap Meet and outsider desert art icon—was kneeling near the pavement spraying foam from a canister, his suspenders stretched across his thin back.

It was too hot for flannel. But under the flannel shirt, a spine. *And under that?*

There was so much to conceal it made me sick.

"Pervert!" I'd said, socking my foot into the pouch of his hip, as close to his groin as I could reach. It was soft. I retracted, weak with something adrenaline-like. He burbled quietly and clutched toward my leg. I pushed him away. As he fell, a small red splotch—*juice?*—popped from his mouth.

"Pervert," I'd repeated, but with less assurance. It seemed like no one had seen. Did anyone ever see anything? I fumbled with the textured door of the cave, panting. Then pulled my selves back in.

"You always put yourself through stuff like this," my girlfriend said through the door, "trying to write."

While working on a story everything was at play, I found it very painful. Even when editing, for instance, if I wanted to change a word I tried to keep as many of the original letters on the screen as I could, fitting them into their replacement so they wouldn't lose their place, get infinitely lost.

"This isn't about a story," I said.

"Oh."

The other me lounged near the tiny calcite lake. The me who believed I was only an imprint of another. That met with the flesh-and-blood world of real dicks and vaginas, I'd disappear.

Completely empty like this, she'd have to leave me.

"I bought a blanket," I said.

When my girlfriend and I fought she went away somewhere, eons away, I couldn't reach her. But on good days, we were together in a bright world and she'd tell me things I'd misremember or get purely at their surface valence but nonetheless love.

Like how my earlobes were long, Buddha-like, she said. Or what it meant that among all life-forms, humans alone were defenseless—vulnerable blobs clothed solely in skin.

The idea of anyone else's biology entering her made me crazy.

"Ever seen a rough diamond?" I said.

I bent down. Breaking crystals from the gluey cave floor, I forced their purple saws into my pockets. I couldn't decide. Had the protective mechanism coiled away inside us somewhere or is it true? The possum has its death, the Mojave snake its bridge, the squid its inky cloud, the Texas horned lizard even shoots blood from its eyes, while we, most evolved—need nothing.

Large Animals

In my sleep I was plagued by large animals—teams of grizzlies, timber wolves, gorillas even came in and out of the mist. Once the now extinct northern white rhino also stopped by. But none of them came as often or with such a ferocious sexual charge as what I, mangling Latin and English as usual, called the Walri. Lying there, I faced them as you would the inevitable. They were massive, tube-shaped, sometimes the feeling was only flesh and I couldn't see the top of the cylinder that masqueraded as a head or tusks or eyes. Nonetheless I knew I was in their presence intuitively. There was no mistaking their skin; their smell was unmistakable too, as was their awful weight.

During these nights (the days seemed to disappear before they even started) I was living two miles from a military testing site. In the early morning and throughout the day the soft, dense sound of bombs filled the valley. It was comforting somehow. Otherwise I was entirely alone.

This seemed a precondition for the Walri—that I should be theirs and theirs only. On the rare occasion that I had an overnight visitor to my desert bungalow the Walri were never around. Then the bears would return in force, maybe even a large local animal like a mountain lion or goat, but no form's density came close to walrus-ness. So I became wary and stopped inviting anyone out to visit at all.

The days, unmemorable, had a kind of habitual slide. I would wake up with the sun and begin cleaning the house. No matter how tightly I'd kept the doors shut the day before, dust and sand and even large pieces of mineral rock seemed to shove their way inside. I swept these into piles. Then the dishes that I barely remembered dirtying—some mornings it was as if the whole artillery of pots and pans had been used in the night by someone else—then the trash (again always full), then some coffee. Eight o'clock.

This work done, I sat in various chairs in the house following the bright but pale blades of light. I was drying out. Oh, an LA friend said somewhat knowingly, from the booze? But I had alcohol with me, plenty of it. It wasn't that. I moved as if preprogrammed. Only later did I realize that my sleep was so soggy that it took strong desert sun to unshrivel me and since it was the middle of winter and the beams were perforce slanted, I'd take all of it I could find.

For lunch I got in my car and drove into town, to the empty parking lot of Las Palmas. There were many Mexican joints along the highway that also functioned as Main Street. I hadn't bothered to try them out. Las Palmas, with its vacant booths, dusty cacti, and combination platter lunch special for $11.99 including $4 house margarita, was fine.

A waitress named Tamara worked there. She seemed like the only one. She wasn't my type—so tall she bent over herself and a bona fide chain-smoker. Sometimes to order you'd have to exit your booth and find her puffing outside. A friend who had borrowed the bungalow before I did told me about Tamara and so if I had a crush at all it was an inherited one that even came with inherited guilt—from having taken her on once he could no longer visit her. Regardless, we barely spoke.

I had things I was supposed to be doing, more work than I could accomplish even if I duct-taped my fists to my laptop, but none of it seemed relevant to my current state. In the afternoons I drove back home slowly, always stopping for six-packs of beer at the Circle K. I enjoyed the task. The beer evaporated once I stuck it in my fridge—it was there and then, it was gone.

My sleeping area was simple: a bed on a plywood platform. A wooden dresser. Built-in closets and a cement floor. At first I would wake up in the night from the sheer flattening silence of the desert. It was impossible that the world still existed elsewhere. After that initial jolt, relief.

Don't you miss it? my same friend said during our weekly telephone chats. But I couldn't explain the euphoria of walking up and down the chilly aisles of Stater Bros. in week-old sweatpants if I wanted, uncounted by life. Would I buy refried or whole beans? This brand or that? It didn't matter, no one cared.

It was in these conditions that the Walri arrived.

* * *

I'd slept as usual for the first few hours, heavily, in a kind of coma state. Then had woken, I thought to pee. But lying there with the gritty sheets braided around me, the violet light that was created from the fly zapper, the desert cold that was entering through the gaps and cracks in the fire's absence—I felt a new form of suffocation.

It wasn't supernatural. I'd also had that. The sense of someone's vast weight sitting on the bed with you or patting your body with ghostly hands. This breathless feeling was larger, as if I was uniformly surrounded by mammoth flesh.

Dream parts snagged at me. Slapping sounds and hose-like alien respiration. I felt I was wrestling within inches of what must be—since I couldn't breathe—the end of my life. Now the lens of my dream panned backward and I saw my opponent in his entirety.

He lay (if that's what you could call it) on my bed, thick and wrinkled, the creases in his hide so deep I could stick my arms between them. His teeth were yellow and as long as my legs.

"I'm sexually dormant," I said aloud to him. "But I want to put my balls in someone's face."

Then somehow light was peeling everything back for dawn.

About a mile from my house there was a Fraternal Order of Eagles club. I knew nothing about their organization except that they also functioned as the town library, with books you could check out and an Internet connection that was less dubious than most. "The Aerie" was small and bundled in fake wood paneling—it had first been a prospector's cabin, or what was around here known as a jackrabbit homestead. From what I could tell this meant squattish buildings with cinder block walls and flat, shed-style roofs that you could claim for cheap.

Sure enough, they had a dusty Mac sitting on a Formica table. I waited as a Wrangler-sheathed man signed out of his EarthLink account. "Okay?" I said. I jumped at the creaky boom of my voice. He nodded. I typed madly for what seemed like an hour. But nothing could explain the mystic weirdness of the night before. And besides this phrase, *"the walrus sucks the meat out by sealing its powerful lips to the organism and withdrawing its piston-like tongue,"* only one thing of note: Walri, unlike most marine mammals—seals or sea lions or even manatees—were not entirely fluent in water. They had to sleep on land.

I pictured walruses dragging themselves up out of the sea. It seemed risky, wholly exposing. And then what? One day grow feet? There was that YouTube video of a walrus giving himself a blow job. He didn't need land for that. Each time he grabbed the tip of his head he sunk down with pleasure, never up.

I drove back home. Even though I was no longer new here, I was still unnerved by the perpetual pedestrian traffic on the highway. How in the middle of a stretch of otherwise desolate road, where cars and trucks, even semis pushed one hundred, a figure would suddenly materialize from the sagebrush or the sandy shoulder and stroll across the four cracked lanes like a featureless blot.

* * *

At home I stood in the shower. Out here, even the water smelled dry. I brushed my teeth and watched my gums bleed down into the drain. The phrase "everything was bothering me and nothing was right" ricocheted around in my head. Was it from a recent novel? It seemed like it must be but I couldn't place it. Anyway, I'd been off reading since I'd arrived.

The phone rang. I had to search around to find it. "This is the FOE," said a guy on the other end.

"The who?"

"The Fraternal Order of Eagles, the FOE," he said. "We noticed you here earlier, and wondered, would you like to be jumped in?"

"I don't think so," I said. I swatted, killing two flies on my arm. "What does that involve?"

"Oh, it's your standard, roughhouse initiation. You know, we've been around since 1898."

"I don't think so," I said, hanging up.

Outside, it was already starting to get dark. I hadn't eaten. The day was shifting and formless but in a way that felt oppositional to my usual lack of structure. I changed my clothes into newer jeans and an indigo shirt—"Canadian tuxedo," I said aloud. Back in the car, I let my eyes blur on the horizon. The flat desert dipped up to my left, toward a broken ridgeline. Prehistoric rain had smoothed the saws of rock and now, as the shadows fell, I couldn't budge the feeling that the entire hillside was walrus-like, the dark creases and clefts rippling and stretchy like skin. Even the plain itself, as it ran to meet the rise, seemed to be brown but as sea—a color I'd seen in the shallow pan of San Francisco Bay. Every now and again a trailer home or Airstream winked out from under a swell, but far off. I rubbed my eyes, the image stayed.

I took my usual booth at Las Palmas but was later than usual and Tamara was just getting off. Something was nagging me. A voice again: "Animals are only animals because they are observed." I guessed that was right: the zoo, the aquarium— even the wildlife park. Out here there was nothing to watch, nothing, at least, that let you watch it.

"What are you doing later?" I asked Tamara. She was transferring my check.

"Nothing much," she said. "I'll probably just walk along the road."

"Huh?" I said. "Is that safe???"

"Doing laundry?" she said. "I think so."

I had been going to ask her if she wanted to sit down for an after-shift drink but I was rattled by what she'd said or what I'd heard.

"Laundry, good idea, me too," I said, dashing my name onto the credit card slip.

That night the walrus brought others. I woke similarly, with a pressure pounding against my gut. I stood to pee. My room was damp, Walri sprawled grotesquely on every surface. I sat back down, pulled the palm-tree-patterned cotton blanket up.

"Not a circle jerk but a circle twerk," the king walrus said.

One week later a letter arrived in the mail. I sat at the table and sliced it open. The kitchen was dirtier now. My sleep kept me so busy I rarely had time to clean it. I shook the envelope. The contents slid out with a bump. Divorce papers. They said I had been married (or was still) to someone named CeCe Bardell. Bardell? Even that confused me—we must not have shared names, I guessed.

I returned to the FOE, a little reluctantly this time. A ten-foot-tall wooden eagle greeted me in the parking lot. I wanted to find out anything about my wife. Tamara was on the computer, her long torso punching up and down as she typed.

I shoved the offending envelope in my pocket.

"Shredded beef enchiladas," she said. It's true, I only ordered one thing.

"Do you want to, uhmmm, get a beer tonight?"

As soon as I said it I began to sweat. My kitchen was full of takeout containers, my room was more like a dock house.

"Okay," she said, clicking between screen after screen of what looked like chat rooms. "Why not."

We took my car and drove back along the road. Here it turned dark at four-thirty so by five p.m. it was stygian night. I watched as my lights swished against the metal siding of the Saloon, the only nearby bar. We didn't stop. My feet were locked—resisting any kind of braking action. My shoulders were rigid too. I had that feeling sometimes—I was one of those hibernating sculptures still waiting to be freed from its rock.

In the passenger seat, Tamara was pulling at her ear, squeezing them back and forth.

"You can smoke in the car," I said, whisking down her window. "Seriously!"

It reminded me of my neighbor, or he wasn't my neighbor but my neighbor's property manager. The houses closest to me on either side were empty but not boarded up. Gary was big and tan with gray feathers of chest hair. He drove a shiny energy saver and checked on things. At dawn when I let out the half-stray cat and rubbed my back against the badly tacked doorframe—Gary was out there smoking. Bomb days were best: the reds rawer, the pinks had more juice. Maybe that's why he'd pointed his windshield west and was playing the car radio as the sun swirled up through the dust.

The pose seemed suicidal.

"'Sup, Gary," I called. Sulfur drifted into my mouth. But he kept thick-necking over the steering wheel, either intentionally not turning around or no sound of mine actually came out.

Now I made a slightly too fast right onto Sherman Hoyt. The beams filled the road and against the pavement—miles of scrubby desert. Someone had starting doing wheelies out there and making huge circles with what sounded like, from my bed platform, their 4x4 trucks. When I first arrived I had been terrified at the thought of a V6 or 8 pulling up in the night.

"This is it?" said Tamara.

The siding on my house was peeling from the constantly whipping sand and my landlord had left hunks of debris scattered all over the premises to cure. At first I had wanted to scour the structure's exterior but now the bedsprings and defunct washing machine just looked like familiar shapes to move around.

"Yep," I said.

"I used to buy weed here," she said, unbending out of the car. She seemed suddenly cheerful. "Nice place."

I unlocked the door, or pretended to. The lock was only about 30 percent functional. Still I went through the motions dutifully, as I had when I left the house. Then I turned on a few lights. But not too many, I didn't want her to really look around. I cleared the small kitchen table and took out a six-pack of Sierra Nevada fresh from the Circle K.

"So what's it like being a lesbian?" Tamara said, her legs extending practically inside the stove.

"Umm," I said, hacking out the beer through my throat tubes.

"I mean yeah," I said, "I've watched all the big films—*Go Fish*, *All Over Me*, what was it? That heroin one."

She looked at me blankly. My neck burned.

"But otherwise, I'm not sure I'd really know?"

"Oh," said Tamara, "huh." She lit up from a Newport pack. "I just thought, I mean, for a guy, isn't your Adam's apple a little small?"

"I've also watched *The L Word*," I offered. Pathetic episode after pathetic episode flashed up. "So I think all in all—yeah, it's pretty good?"

But Tamara was on her knees yanking at a piece of plywood floor patch and it seemed like she was barely listening.

"They used to keep extra pot in here," she said as she lifted the board. "Those assholes, but now it's gone."

Beer, I loved it. I opened another one. I gave myself little lobotomies every night just so I could sleep.

"Hey, should we get really fucking drunk?" I said.

The toilet was rushing. I went to jiggle it. I flicked the light switch. Nothing but more blackness—the way that blackness seemed to swell when you tried to amend it. I went out into the cramped hall and toggled that switch as well.

Blacker.

My head felt hazy but I was sober enough to remember that Tamara had gone home after six-pack number two. That we had only approached drunk. That she had started not only pulling at the floorboards but also prowling around the casings of the walls.

"Well-informed guesses!" she'd said.

But I'd become worried about the Walri—would they come? Wouldn't they come? Would they share what we'd been doing?—and so I ushered her out.

I entered the den that also housed the only table and the kitchen. None of those switches worked either. The bungalow's back windows stared toward what, in a thin string along the highway, was town. I lifted a dusty shade. Nothing punctured the dark for miles and miles. Even the stadium lights with their big sodium flares were dead.

I pushed on a flashlight. My divorce papers lay on the table with crazy faces—tongues sticking out and googly eyes—drawn over the back of them in Sharpie; "302-897-3356," it also said.

Tamara answered immediately.

"Do you remember a guy who used to come into Las Palmas, about my height, black bangs, glasses?" I said. "A real painterly dude."

"I guess so?" she said.

"Well did you like him? Don't bother bullshitting!"

I flicked a switch up and down helplessly. No result.

"If you're worried about this blackout," she said, "it's normal. The bases out here cut power whenever they want."

Was I worried about the blackout? It hadn't occurred to me. I had only wanted to call her to ask my burning question. Now it had been asked.

"Good night," I said.

I slept but woke often to breathing. I knew it wasn't mine and yet also no one was there. The sounds were heavy, lactation-like. As if moisture was being added to and then sucked from the room with a shop vac. I heard a tap-tapping on the window. I pulled back the sheet that acted as a curtain. No one. I lay my head back down.

Go back to sleep, I told my thoughts.

All the old tricks: the systematically drawing my mind toward everyone I had ever known so I could protect them with ad hoc language spells, the ticking off of sex partners as half my brain worked overtime batting away something uglier . . . I touched the front of my throat. *Why had Tamara said that?*

The rapping again. This time harder. Please, I said.

But something more incredible was happening. I pushed my face up against the nonoperable window then walked trancelike to the door.

Rain, in the Mojave.

In the morning gullies were slicing into the drought-compacted sand and threatening slides. White foam washed over the road. There weren't drains or gutters. Nothing seemed ready to absorb.

With fog on the Sierras, the landscape entered another dimension. The ridgelines I had come to know as fixed disappeared or traded with each other and when the sun smoked through they steamed like treeless Herzogian jungle plots.

Water. Even the air suddenly had weight—you had to enter it before you moved past.

There was a baked riverbed that ran by the back of my house. Once, feeling jammed-in indoors, I had walked along its packed floor. The bed bent south. A mile down I came to a huge trash bag. Don't be a body, I said. I couldn't help myself. Toeing it, my foot against the plastic made a fleshy thud. I knelt down and pulled at the bag's edge. The muzzle of a large dog fell out. A husky maybe, or something part wolf. I imagined a highway hit-and-run, the dead stop, then guilty tracks back to do *this*. I tried to re-cover the open face but that seemed worse.

Now brown sludge trickled against the riverbed's walls. The blackout and the rain were, I believed, connected.

I moved along the bungalow's perimeter, looking at the pools of water. Athel pines brushed my neck, heavy and salty.

Wetness stained their under-branches in splotches. I was standing near an outshed I had always considered a spider hole when Gary came by.

"You okay?" he said.

I jumped.

He joggled his plastic cup that I could only guess contained grape soda and a sizable dump of Everclear.

I moved away from a circle of rocks I had been staring at. They seemed placed intentionally, by guided hands. I believed in talismans, energy fields, alien skirts of light.

"Going to the VFW tonight?" he said.

Would Tamara be there? flashed before I could control it.

"Mmmm," I said. "It's?"

"Taco Wednesdays."

Every week Gary came by to ask me and every week, I, or my passive body, declined.

"I'll try," I said.

The VFW was a bigger club than the FOE. With the bases so close by, wives or husbands of service members were always looking for something to do. Sunday breakfasts, holiday raffles—the weekly tacos pulled everyone in, desert rat or commando, because the ground-beef-filled shells were only fifty cents each.

Dressing again, I felt self-conscious in the mirror. I tugged on my Vibram-treaded boots. Took them off. Shoved them back on. I wasn't sure I liked mingling with the army crowd. Everyone had black wraparounds and a fresh don't-fuck-with-me barbershop fade.

The light was dulling. I walked out to the carport. My car clicked to life. From my road, Utah Trail, I spun the wheel left. A hitchhiker stood there with a cardboard placard: "Tacos ☺." He was thumbing toward town. This way was only more desert. NO SERVICES FOR 100 MILES, said a sign—blurring from sudden green to pitch-black.

The road had an oily sheen but the rain had stopped. Black air hugged black desert and sometimes a low span of hill glowed. I'd just drive a little, I thought, before making my decision. Sometimes I did this—drove out. Each time I felt euphoric pushing away from home. Then I realized the road kept on going and going—that there was no natural end or climax. Always I'd pick an unremarkable place—a nothing shoulder, a tiny shack or caved-in mailbox as my turn-around point.

I pulled to the side. This was Wonder Valley, where nothing seemed to live at all. I pressed open the door. Big scraping sounds were moving across the bottom of the foothills. Carpet bombing at low altitudes. The wet desert smelled musty and like gas.

Taco night loomed. I dialed Tamara's number into my cell without sending. *So what about Tamara?* Or, for that matter, CeCe Bardell?

I uncrumpled the divorce papers and tried to read them. It was dark and smoky. I could barely work out CeCe's note through the marker stain of Tamara's teenage-like digits. *"Yes I've been fucking Tim. Ever since he came back from the desert. But how can you possibly blame me??? After all, YOUR..."* I shoved the wad in the glove box and turned the car around, slowly accelerating. It had been this way all my life—a desperation I couldn't extricate myself from. I hated being seen.

* * *

I blew through a stop sign, it didn't matter, everyone did it. A sign emerged: ENTERING . . . I was close to Sherman Hoyt, I could just as easily turn home. But as I passed my turnoff, my car jerked horribly, making a gross sack-like crunch.

I stopped in the middle of the lane. I was breathing loudly as if I'd been running. Whatever it had been was big.

I could barely get out of the car. I knew I should search around in the brush or roadside ditch. There'd been—at the last minute—a recognizable weight. I felt the reverberations in my body, how I felt the whole world there sometimes. My arm seemed welded, the door lock, locked. It was raining again. I could see at least that nothing was in front of my headlights. I reversed anyway, the car worked. I turned on my blinker and didn't pull over again until the VFW.

"Hey," said Tamara. She was wearing a fringe vest, she looked good.

"Blackout still going, huh?" I said.

They were running on giant generators; only that could account for the blaze of light.

But it was as if I couldn't really focus. She was sitting with her hand on a guy from the FOE—he raised up his beer, shoved back his hat, did what people in his position did.

It barely mattered.

I knew about the bloodied body that would meet me at home. How I would hold him—still damp, rub his slabs of flesh, stare into his flat lids.

"Wouldn't *you* sleep in water," I said, to the table of them, "if you could?"

I was sore all over. I walked to the overfull line that butted the dinky kitchenette, nodding to all the Garys and their cups of Everclear on my way.

"Can I please have a taco," I said.

Acknowledgments

There's no way this book would be here without my family, who besides giving me the space and trust to do this, make conjuring other worlds feel possible. This book was made not apart from family, but because of it, in all its many shades.

Thank you to my grandmothers, who loved reading most. To my magic brother Thomas, who might be younger but is teaching me everything, including how to have a euphoric body. To my empathic and deep-seeing mom and undauntable dad, who themselves lead unexampled lives, and who let me be myself and love me for it. Always. To my Waldron family, especially "Special Lady" crew Sonja, Iris, + Avery. Also K Keller and Starla. And the small animals I know best: Wally, Beulah, and Lucha.

Thank you to Amy Sillman, for this transformative cover, and for making me more lumpen. To Susan Miller, whose genius perfectly joins the scatological and sacred. To my story incubator + therapist Jodi Panas, who I know will be reading this. To my heart guards, Lanka Tattersall and Lauryn Siegel. To Nicco Beretta, who among so many things, is writing an essential book. To Cole Snyder for a whole life of rescues. To Lynne Angel, above all, for getting it.

Thank you to my conspirators + inspirators: Corrine Fitzpatrick. Sara Marcus, Matt Longabucco, Dia Felix, Krystal Languell, Ann Stephenson, the Herrings en swarm, Justin Torres, Michelle Tea, Dorthe Nors, John Coletti, Diana Cage, Caroline Bergvall, Nicole Eisenman, Camille Roy, Amy Scholder, and to Christina Crosby—who's right there underneath. To Laurie Weeks for the astral dust. To Lynne Tillman for telling me you have to love it. To Jason Daniel Schwartz for going there with me and farther.

Thank you to Maggie Nelson, for helping at every corner and curve—whose own writing is a beacon, and who without, this book wouldn't have happened.

To my brilliant and intrepid editor, Julie Buntin—I'm so lucky your sense of things is joyous and porous enough to let this book slip in. Thank you especially for your steady hand, capacious trust, and every scrap of ornament we cut.

To Marya Spence for your sagacity and this beautiful risk.

To Andy Hunter + Catapult—I can't believe how cool you are. You continue to set a new bar with your intelligence and sight.

Thank you to Sara Jaffe, who did it with me, each step, forever reader and forever pal.

And to Litia Perta, you are in every beat of this. I love you. Thank you for the wildness of your knowing and for all of the unknowing still to come.

About the Author

Jess Arndt received her MFA at the Milton Avery Graduate School of the Arts at Bard College, and was a 2013 Graywolf SLS Fellow and 2010 Fiction Fellow at the New York Foundation of the Arts. Her writing has appeared in *Fence, Bomb, Aufgabe, Parkett,* and *Night Papers,* and as an action text with the Knife's Shaking the Habitual world tour. She is a co-founder of New Herring Press, and lives and works in Los Angeles.